Book Six:

Blast from the Past

Books by MEG CABOT

FOR TEENS

For a complete list of Meg Cabot's books,
please visit www.megcabot.com

MEG CABOT

Allie Finkle's RULES for GIRLS

Book Six:

Blast from the Past

SCHOLASTIC PRESS · NEW YORK

An Imprint of Scholastic Inc.

Library of Congress Cataloging-in-Publication Data Available

ISBN 978-0-545-04048-8

10 9 8 7 6 5 4 3 2 1

Printed in the U.S.A.   23
First edition, September 2010

The display type was set in Chaloops and Yellabelly.
The text type was set in Centaur MT Regular.
Book design by Elizabeth B. Parisi

*For my old friends <u>and</u> my
new friends . . . and friends
I haven't even made yet*

Many thanks to Laura Langlie
and Abigail McAden

RULE #1

No Cell Phones Until You're in the Sixth Grade

Our across-the-street neighbors went on a cruise for a week, so they asked me to pick up their newspaper and mail every day while they were gone.

This was a job that required *a lot* of responsibility.

But I never missed a day. Not even when it rained so much one day that the wall in Mark's closet started cracking, and then bubbling, and then finally burst open because of all the water that was trickling down inside it from a leak in our roof.

That day, I just put on my raincoat and boots and went and got the Aronoffs' newspaper and mail in the rain like it was nothing.

So you can imagine my complete surprise when the

Aronoffs got home from their cruise and gave me ten dollars because they were so impressed by the great job I had done neatly stacking their mail and newspapers in their front hallway while they were gone.

Honestly, I would have done it for free. *It's important to be nice to your neighbors,* so that when you do something such as accidentally run over their azaleas while practicing skidding to a sudden stop on your bike like a girl motocross racer, they won't be as mad at you.

That's a rule.

Anyway, that ten dollars plus the twenty-six dollars I'd already saved up from my allowance for doing chores around the house meant that I had thirty-six dollars.

And thirty-six dollars is enough to buy a lot of things.

Such as a cell phone.

"I thought your parents said you couldn't have a cell phone until you were in the sixth grade," my uncle Jay said when I asked him to come over and take me to the mall so I could buy my new cell phone.

"But it's my own money," I explained. "I'm allowed to buy anything I want with my own money."

That's a rule. Or at least it should be.

I'd been wanting my own cell phone for as long as I could remember. I knew lots of kids in the fourth grade — like my friend Rosemary — who had their own cell phones.

My parents wouldn't let me get one because they said that I was too young and hadn't shown that I was responsible enough to own one (especially given what had happened with my Nintendo DS).

But it wasn't like I had ever really liked my Nintendo that much in the first place. I enjoy games that require a stretchy imagination more than games that require stretchy thumbs.

My parents say *Losing electronic devices is irresponsible.* If we lose ours, we have to buy new ones with our own money.

Both my brothers have been extremely careful not to lose their Nintendos ever since they found out about this rule.

But if you ask me, this rule isn't fair. Mom and Dad didn't even tell us this rule until *after* I'd lost my Nintendo.

I said, "Telling someone that something is a rule after they've already broken that rule without knowing it was a rule in the first place isn't fair."

But my dad said, *"Ignorance of the law is no excuse."*

Whatever that means.

Anyway, I don't believe I'm not responsible enough to own a cell phone. I nursed a tiny kitten — my cat, Mewsie — practically from death into healthy young feline adulthood.

And okay, yes, I lost my Nintendo.

But that is just a handheld game-playing device! I wouldn't lose something important like a cell phone. I actually *need* one of those (even though Mom says I don't). I have a lot of important calls to make.

Like to my mom if, for instance, my little brother Kevin (whom I have to walk to and from school every day) ever happens to fall down an air shaft in a freak accident and break his leg, or something.

This could totally happen.

And having enough money to buy the phone myself definitely shows that I'm responsible enough to own one!

4

"I don't even think you can get a cell phone for thirty-six dollars," Uncle Jay said.

"Yes," I said. "You can. I saw one in the store the other day for less than that."

"But that's just the cost of the phone," Uncle Jay said. "You also have to pay for the calling plan."

"The what?" I had no idea what he was talking about.

"You have to pay for every call you make and every text you send, in addition to the cost of the phone. Look, I don't mind taking you to the mall," Uncle Jay said, "but I want to make sure your parents are okay with this plan of yours before we go."

"Don't worry," I said. "They will be."

The only problem was, my mom wasn't.

"What?" She pushed some hair back behind one ear.

I'll admit Mom was kind of distracted.

Because she was holding a flashlight for my dad as he lay with his head in a hole in my brother Mark's closet, looking at the dry rot they had discovered inside the wall, which also turned out to be inside all the walls of the entire upstairs of our house.

"I have thirty-six dollars of my own money," I explained again very quickly. "So now Uncle Jay is going to take me to the mall to buy a cell phone. I'll be home in time for dinner. Bye!"

"Ouch!" Dad said as he hit his head trying to crawl out of the hole.

"Can I go inside the wall next?" Kevin wanted to know. He was sitting with Mark on the bottom bed of the bunks the two of them used to share in our old house, but that had been split apart now that they both had separate rooms.

"No," Mom said, switching off the flashlight.

"But I'm the smallest," Kevin said.

"He is," Mark agreed. "He could tell you how far back the dry rot goes."

"*No one,*" Dad said, crawling out from the closet, "*goes in the wall.* That's a rule."

"I saw snails when I looked in there before," Mark reported. "Also mushrooms."

"Good God," Mom said.

"We could make a casserole," Uncle Jay suggested.

"Okay," I said. "Well, I'll be seeing you."

"Wait," Mom asked. Her eyes focused on me, and not in a good way. "Where did you say you were going?"

"I told you," I said. "To the mall to buy a cell phone. And you can't say no, because I'm doing it with my own money."

"Hey," Kevin said. "I want a cell phone, too."

"Me, too," Mark said. "No fair."

"That's enough," Mom snapped.

Moms don't snap too often.

But when they do, you had better stop whatever you were doing wrong, if you know what's good for you. That's a rule.

"All of you," Mom said. "Just stop it." She pointed at me. "You know the rules. No cell phones until you're in the sixth grade."

"But, Mom!" I couldn't believe it. Well, I guess I sort of could, under the circumstances. But still.

"We agreed you wouldn't be allowed to have a cell phone until you were in sixth grade," she said. "And then only if you can show you're responsible enough."

"But, Mom," I said. "I *did* show I'm responsible enough! It's my money. I earned it picking up the Aronoffs' mail

7

and newspapers and doing chores around the house. *If I earned the money, I should be able to spend it on whatever I want. That's the rule.*"

Or at least, that *should* be the rule.

"Not if you're spending it on something that we already discussed you're not allowed to have until you're older," Mom said. "Trying to trick your uncle into taking you to the store so that you can buy something we've forbidden you to own just proves that fact. It's hardly what I'd call responsible behavior."

Was this true? I wasn't sure. I mean . . . it *was* my money.

And I *did* ask permission.

Uncle Jay looked down at me. I knew I couldn't blame him for how all of my dreams of being a cell phone owner were crashing and burning down around me. He'd been very supportive, offering to drive me to the store in his car — which doubles as his pizza delivery vehicle, so it always smells faintly of pepperoni — and everything. Even if he *had* said he'd only do it if Mom and Dad said it was okay.

"Sorry, kid," Uncle Jay said. "Those are the rules."

"Yeah, well," I muttered. "Sometimes the rules are stupid."

"What was that, Allie?" my mom asked in a dangerous voice.

"Nothing," I said.

But it was true. Apparently, it wasn't enough to pick up a neighbor's mail during a rainstorm, or to raise a kitten, or to walk a six-year-old brother back and forth to school.

How was it that I was responsible enough to do all those things, but not responsible enough to spend my own money (that I had earned) on the things that I wanted . . . or even needed?

When were my parents *ever* going to think I was responsible enough? Sixth grade?

But that was *two whole years away*.

They might as well have said "never."

RULE #2

Cheyenne O'Malley Is the Most Popular
Girl in Room 209, and Probably
in the Whole World . . . at Least in
Her Own Mind

I was still mad about the whole cell phone thing during the walk to school the next morning.

"The worst part of it was," I said to my friends, "that last night at dinner, nobody would even talk about it. All anybody could talk about was dry rot."

My friend Sophie sucked in her breath.

"You have dry rot in your house?" she asked. "Allie, that's super serious! Your whole house could collapse in a pile of rubble with all of you inside of it if you don't get it fixed right away." Sophie loves disasters of any kind, medical, man-made, or natural, and especially likes reading about them, then describing them to us in graphic detail whenever she gets the opportunity. "Didn't you guys have an inspection before you moved in?"

"How should I know?" I shrugged. "When we moved in, I thought the stupid house was haunted. That's what your brother told me, anyway." I narrowed my eyes at my friend Erica, who lives next door.

"I'm sorry," Erica said, looking apologetic. "You know John. He loves to tease people."

I smiled to show I hadn't meant to be snotty. I was just in a bad mood about the cell phone.

"Well," I said. "It turned out to be a leak, not ghosts. The roof people are coming today to see if they can fix it."

"And if I'm home when they come, Mom said I could help them with the inspection," Kevin declared.

"Yeah," I said, rolling my eyes. "Right, Kevin."

My walking Kevin to and from kindergarten every day leads to his listening in on all my conversations with my friends. Kevin thinks my friends actually like him, which is an incorrect assumption. Although they do sometimes fight over who gets to hold his hand on the way to school, so you could see why he might think this.

But this is only because none of them has a little brother, and has no idea what a pain they can be.

"I'm sure you'll be a big help to the roof inspectors, Kevin," Erica assured Kevin kindly.

"Oh, I know I will," Kevin said. "They'll probably give me one of their hard hats."

I sincerely hoped this was not true. Otherwise, Kevin was going to insist on wearing that hard hat to kindergarten every day until school let out for summer, just like he'd insisted on wearing his pirate costume every day for almost the entire first semester, thus making the Finkle family the biggest laughingstock of the entire student body of Pine Heights Elementary.

"Don't feel bad, Allie," my friend Caroline said. "Having a cell phone isn't that great, really."

Only a person who has a cell phone, like Caroline, would say this.

"My mom said I could have my sister Missy's old cell phone," Erica admitted. When I looked at her with my eyes widened, she added hastily, "But now I'm going to tell her I don't want it. What's the point if I can't text my best friend?"

She put an arm around my neck and hugged me. Erica always tries to make everyone around her feel better.

"Well," Sophie said. "I'm not sure I particularly want a cell phone, since some research shows their use increases brain cancer in teens and children. But even if I did want one, my dad says I can't have one anyway until I start remembering not to leave things in the pockets of my jeans when I put them in the wash. Like my iPod. So I know what you mean, Allie, about being responsible. It's not fair. My mom was so distracted over her PhD the other day that she left her laptop on the roof of the car and drove all around town with it like that, until someone finally told her when she was stopped at a red light. But my dad didn't say *she* couldn't have a cell phone."

I shook my head. Life is so unfair. Like brain cancer.

By the time we got to Pine Heights, we were all thoroughly depressed. Except for Rosemary, who came running up to us on the playground (she lives in the suburbs, and so she gets to take the bus to school instead of walking, like we do. The lucky duck. It's always been my dream to ride on a school bus, since I've never ever gotten to, my parents always having made the poor decision of moving to within walking distance of every school I've ever gone to) to show us the new game she'd downloaded to her cell phone.

"It's so cool, you guys," she said excitedly.

It was hard to get as pumped as she was, however, when I didn't have a cell phone to be able to download games to.

It was right then that Cheyenne O'Malley sauntered up with her best friends, Marianne and Dominique (or M and D, as she refers to them), texting away on *her* cell phone. *Cheyenne O'Malley is the most popular girl in Room 209, and probably in the whole world . . . at least in her own mind.*

This is pretty much a rule.

"Oh," Cheyenne said, looking down her nose at Rosemary's phone. "You girls still play video games? Aren't those for babies? I would have thought you'd have outgrown those by now."

Then she and M and D sauntered away, laughing and texting one another.

We had to hold Rosemary back to keep her from pounding Cheyenne's delicate face into the grass.

"I only want to hurt her a little," Rosemary said.

We assured her it wasn't worth it. Even though the truth is, I actually think it might have been.

Things started to look up a little, though, when we sat down at our desks and Mrs. Hunter, our teacher, walked up in front of Room 209 and said she had a very special announcement.

Mrs. Hunter is not only the best teacher I've ever had — who once said that I acted like a mature professional and that I'm a joy to have around the classroom — she's also the prettiest, even though she has short hair. Mrs. Hunter wears eyeliner to match her green eyes, and sparkly lip gloss, which she reapplies at her desk when she thinks no one is looking (but I'm always looking, because Mrs. Hunter makes me sit in the last row next to her desk with all the worst boys in our entire class. This is because she says I'm a positive influence on them).

Plus, Mrs. Hunter wears stylish clothes, like high-heeled zip-up boots with skirts that are a length my mom said she gave up after college, but good for Mrs. Hunter if she can still carry it off.

So even though I had thirty-six dollars of my very own but I couldn't spend it on what I wanted because my mom says I'm not very responsible, and the walls of my house were full of mushrooms and snails and, according to Sophie, were going to collapse on me without warning, and probably my little brother was going to start wearing a hard hat to school every day, continuing to humiliate me in the eyes of the entire student body for the rest of the school year, at least *one* good thing was going to happen.

Because *When a teacher like Mrs. Hunter says she has an announcement, you know it's going to be something exciting.*

That was a rule.

Today was no exception.

"Class," Mrs. Hunter said, tucking her short skirt beneath her as she settled onto her favorite stool in front of us. "I have something very exciting to announce: Room Two Oh Nine is going on a field trip!"

RULE #3

Asking Teachers About Their Boyfriends Is Against the Rules

The minute Mrs. Hunter said we were going on a field trip, everyone in Room 209 went bananas.

Because Room 209 had never been on a field trip before. At least not while I had been there.

The girls all squealed with delight. The boys all fist-bumped one another. Patrick Day, who sits on the end of my row, jumped up on top of his desk and played air guitar until Rosemary pulled him down by the belt loops of his jeans. Stuart Maxwell, who sits on one side of me, started making farting noises with his armpit, and Joey Fields, who sits on my other side, began barking like a dog.

It took all my powers of being a positive influence to get them both to settle down.

The truth was, however, I was pretty excited myself . . . due to one simple but totally embarrassing fact:

I had never been on a field trip before.

I know. Amazing, but true.

It wasn't that my old school, Walnut Knolls Elementary, hadn't taken us on any field trips.

It was just that every single time, something had happened on the day of the trip to prevent me from being able to go.

Not something that had to do with me being irresponsible, either. At least, not in my opinion.

Like the time in first grade when my class got to go to the ice-skating rink as a very special prize for not talking in line on the way to the art and music rooms all semester?

I got the chicken pox.

Getting the chicken pox was *not* my fault. That can happen to anyone.

And the time in second grade, when my class was scheduled to go to the state park to learn about nature preservation?

The day before we were supposed to go, there was an unprecedented flooding event, so all the trails in the park were washed out for the season, and the trip was canceled.

How was that *my* fault? I can't control the weather.

But okay, the thing in third grade? In third grade our whole class was supposed to take a bus into the city to go to the Children's Museum.

This was a very big deal because the SpaceQuest planetarium (with a DigiStar sky projection system . . . in 3-D) had just opened there.

And so had the Dinosphere, where you get to explore what it was like during the Cretaceous period more than sixty-five million years ago.

But what was most important, it had an exhibit of rare collectible Barbies. Not that I cared about *that*. I mean, very much.

I was very excited, just in general, about going to the Children's Museum.

So was my best friend, Mary Kay Shiner. Mary Kay was so excited about it that she said I should give *her* my signed permission slip to hand in, because back then I had a slight tendency to lose things (not like now. I'm very responsible about those kinds of things *now*). She wanted to be especially sure I wouldn't make the colossal mistake of losing something as important as the signed permission slip to go to the Children's Museum with the rest of our class.

I never imagined at the time that Mary Kay and I would have a big fight (even though throughout our entire friendship, we fought every day) and that Mary Kay would hand in *her* permission slip, but accidentally on purpose *forget to hand in mine* . . .

. . . something I wouldn't find out until the *morning of the field trip,* when it was too late to do anything about it, because my parents had taken Kevin to Big and Small Lots to buy giant rolls of paper towels, which is a store *outside of their cell phone provider's network,* so my teacher couldn't reach them.

So where was I while my class was having fun watching the wonders of the universe at the planetarium in the Children's Museum (in 3-D glasses), and being chased by animatronic dinosaurs, and seeing rare collectible Barbies?

I was sitting in the Walnut Knolls Elementary School principal's office, drawing pictures of dogs with Mrs. Jones, the principal's administrative assistant (although she *did* say I draw excellent pictures of dogs, which is true. They're based on my own dog, Marvin).

Mary Kay and I became friends again, of course. Because after she came back from her super fun day at the Children's Museum, she cried and said she was sorry and begged me to forgive her.

Mom and Dad said that it was really *my* fault for being so irresponsible as to trust something as important as a permission slip to somebody as flaky (and, frankly, mean) as Mary Kay.

But if you ask me, I just have the worst field trip luck of anyone. It's pretty much a rule that *If there's going to be a field trip and Allie Finkle is scheduled to go on it, you can just count her out.*

But not this time. The minute I heard Mrs. Hunter say

the words "field" and "trip," I knew this was going to be different.

Because now, in fourth grade, I was finally, *finally* going to get to go on a field trip! I was responsible enough now that I knew I wasn't going to let anything stand in my way. I didn't even care *where* we were going . . . just so long as I was going to get to go *somewhere*.

And on a bus! A real school bus!

Of course . . . I never *had* gotten to go to the Children's Museum, much less see that exhibit of rare collectible Barbies (which had turned out to be a traveling exhibit, and had left the city shortly after my class had seen it).

But maybe this was going to be my lucky chance! Maybe the Barbie exhibit had come back!

Of course the minute the chattering, farting noises, and barking died down, Cheyenne O'Malley's hand shot up into the air.

"Um, excuse me, Mrs. Hunter?" she said.

Mrs. Hunter heaved a tiny sigh. Probably only I heard it. Because I hear everything Mrs. Hunter does.

"Yes, Cheyenne?" she asked.

"I'd like to nominate where we go on our class field trip," Cheyenne said, putting her arm down.

I didn't know we could nominate where we could go! If so, I wanted to nominate the Barbie exhibit.

"Cheyenne," Mrs. Hunter said, "that's already been decided."

Cheyenne looked furious.

"But we never even got any say in the matter!" she said. "And it's my understanding that the new Taylor Swift movie is opening this weekend at the mall!"

"Well, Cheyenne," Mrs. Hunter said patiently as M and D and the rest of the girls in Room 209 sucked in their breath eagerly, while the boys made various noises in imitation of throwing up or gagging at the idea of going to a Taylor Swift movie. "That is very interesting. However —"

It was right then that something hit one of the classroom windows.

Not hard enough to break it. Just hard enough to make

a sharp *RAP!* noise. Not *SMACK!* or *THUD!* like the body of a bird accidentally flying into the windows would, either.

Everyone looked over at the windows.

That's when it happened again. *RAP!*

"Hey," Stuart Maxwell yelled. "Someone's shooting at the windows!"

"Naw," Patrick Day said knowledgeably. Because he has a BB gun. "That's just rocks."

Of course everyone jumped up from their seats and hurried over to the windows to see who would be throwing rocks at our classroom windows, even though Mrs. Hunter was saying, "Class, please remain in your seats. I'll take care of this."

When we got to the windows and looked down into the playground, we were disappointed to see a tall man with brown hair, wearing a suit and carrying a small suitcase (not a SWAT outfit and carrying a machine gun), reaching down to pick up another handful of gravel at the bottom of the flagpole to throw at our windows. When he looked up and saw all of us pressing our faces to the windows, he straightened, smiled, and waved at us in a very excited way.

We waved back automatically.

"Who is he?" everyone wanted to know. "Why is he throwing gravel at our windows?"

"He looks nice," a lot of the girls said.

"He's crazy," several of the boys said. "Maybe he's homeless."

"But he has a suitcase," the girls said.

"He's not homeless," Mrs. Hunter said. She looked like she was trying not to laugh. "He's just an old friend who's being very silly."

Mrs. Hunter waved for her silly old friend to leave. He put both hands over his chest and staggered around the flagpole like his heart was breaking and he was dying. I tried not to laugh, just like Mrs. Hunter. But it was hard not to. Even Mrs. Hunter was smiling, though she looked like she was trying to keep her expression disapproving as she pulled the string to lower the blinds.

Everyone groaned. We wanted to see what Mrs. Hunter's silly old friend would do next.

"Go back to your seats, everyone," Mrs. Hunter said. But she was still smiling. "The show is over. I'm sorry for that interruption. My friend was just trying to be funny."

"Mrs. Hunter," Cheyenne asked. "Was that your boyfriend?"

I was kind of shocked that Cheyenne asked that. *Asking teachers about their boyfriends is against the rules*, I thought. I was glad when Mrs. Hunter said, "I'm afraid that's none of your business, Cheyenne."

Then as we were all taking our seats again and Mrs. Hunter went on to explain how attending the new Taylor Swift movie was never going to be something she'd have considered us doing as a class during school hours because of its lack of educational merit, I wondered if Mrs. Hunter *did* have a boyfriend. I knew she was divorced, and that she had a little son.

But she was also very pretty, and not that old. At least, not as old as my mom.

So why *wouldn't* Mrs. Hunter have a boyfriend?

And why *wouldn't* he be funny, and do something like

throw rocks at her classroom window to show her how much he liked her? Boys do even weirder things than that to show girls that they like them, such as try to wipe boogers on them.

Still, it was weird to think of Mrs. Hunter with a boyfriend. Did Mrs. Hunter go on dates, like to the movies and restaurants and stuff, like Erica's older sister, Missy, says *she's* going to do, just as soon as she meets a boy who isn't completely immature and likes gymnastics as much as she does?

I don't know why, but the thought of Mrs. Hunter going on dates with the man from the flagpole made me feel weird.

"Psst." Rosemary was leaning back in her chair and whispering to me. She, too, had been relegated to the last row in our class in the hopes of being a positive influence. Although I suspect mainly it's because she's way bigger than Patrick, Stuart, and Joey. "I think you're finally going to get to ride on a *BUS*."

"I know," I whispered back. This was much better than thinking about Mrs. Hunter's maybe boyfriend.

"Where do you think we're gonna go?" Rosemary asked.

"Honeypot," Patrick Day, who sits on the other side of Rosemary, whispered to us out of the side of his mouth.

"If you ever call me that again, I'll make you eat this," Rosemary said, showing him the side of her fist.

Patrick looked bored. "No. I meant the one-room *school-house* at Honeypot *Prairie*. We just started that unit on pioneer settlers to our area, remember? When Mrs. Danielson's class next door started *their* unit on pioneer settlers, *they* had to go to Honeypot Prairie. So why wouldn't we?"

Rosemary and I exchanged horrified glances.

And sure enough, the next thing we knew, Mrs. Hunter was saying, "Class, for our field trip this Friday, we'll be going to Honeypot Prairie to visit their restored one-room schoolhouse and living history museum that re-creates the lives of the pioneer settlers to our area."

RULE #4

Living History Museums
Are Just Awful

No. This could *not* be happening.

Not on top of the cell phone thing with my mom, and Mrs. Hunter and her maybe possible boyfriend.

Because Honeypot Prairie, according to what we'd heard from all the kids in Room 208, the other fourth-grade class at Pine Heights Elementary School, is supposed to be totally boring.

Well, what *wouldn't* be boring compared to the Children's Museum, with its SpaceQuest planetarium (with DigiStar sky projection system that shows you all the wonders of the universe . . . in 3-D!), but also the Dinosphere, where real (animatronic) dinosaurs actually try to attack you as you walk down a path through a jungle simulated to be exactly like it was during the Cretaceous period more than sixty-five million years ago.

Not only that, but they've got a thirteen-foot-tall giant beating heart you can actually walk through in order to learn how all the ventricles and arteries and stuff actually connect (important for me to know as someone who wants to be a veterinarian slash actress someday) in their You and Your Body exhibit.

I know all this because my ex-best friend, Mary Kay, told me all about it after she got back from the field trip I missed because of her losing my permission slip. Mary Kay said it was amazing (she said the Barbie exhibit was the best thing of all. You could interactively design your own Barbie or Ken).

They don't have *anything* 3-D or animatronic at Honeypot Prairie. According to Mrs. Danielson's class, all they have at Honeypot Prairie are people dressed in old-timey clothes, who talk in old-timey talk, refusing to answer the simplest question like, "Where is the bathroom?" without going, "Well, there, young feller. If you want to take a bath, you have to pay five cents to do it at the grand hotel!

That's the only tub in town. But if it's ye olde water closet you're talkin' about, you'll find it down the milking trail, behind the bake house, but to the right of the ye olde covered bridge!"

Oh, okay. Thanks for that. That explains everything.

And that's not even mentioning Ye Olde Blacksmith Shoppe or the fact that according to the kids in Mrs. Danielson's class, there hadn't been a juice box to be found on the *entire property*.

I wasn't sure even the fun of riding a bus for the very first time would be worth that.

Let's face it. *Living history museums are totally boring.*

"At Honeypot Prairie," Mrs. Hunter said while we stared at her in stunned silence, "we're going to learn how to shoe a horse, make bread from scratch, and build a wigwam, just like the pioneers and Native Americans from our area that we've been reading about!"

Rosemary and I looked at each other with skeptically raised eyebrows. It was true we'd been learning about this stuff in class.

But who needs to know how to make bread when you

can very easily buy it in a store, already sliced and fortified with many vitamins and minerals?

I would way rather have been chased by a fake dinosaur.

"At Honeypot's one-room schoolhouse," Mrs. Hunter said, "we'll read aloud from the recitation bench and copy math problems from the board onto our own slates, just like children in the eighteen fifties used to, because books and paper were too expensive and very rare in those days. We'll even learn how to make our own kick balls!"

An interactive game in which you could design your own kick ball didn't sound *so* bad.

"Because, as we've been learning," Mrs. Hunter went on, "often children would make their own toys. By wrapping any leftover string or twine they could find around and around a rock, and then covering it with a piece of fabric, they would make a kick ball, like the ones you use on the playground at recess!"

Rosemary, who'd been leaning her chair on its back legs, abruptly lowered it to all four feet with a thump.

It was clear from her expression that there was *no way* she was going to enjoy making a kick ball from string and a rock. That was a little *too* interactive.

I knew exactly how Rosemary felt.

And I thought *my* parents were harsh for not letting me have a cell phone. The pioneer kids had it *way* harsher.

Cheyenne shoved her hand into the air.

"Excuse me, Mrs. Hunter," she said.

"Yes, Cheyenne," Mrs. Hunter said, sounding a bit tired.

"It's my understanding," Cheyenne said, "that when Mrs. Danielson's class went to Honeypot Prairie, they were encouraged to wear period clothing. Will we, too, be encouraged to wear period clothing?"

Period clothing? I would just like to say that no one has to wear period clothing when they go to the Children's Museum.

"That's a good point," Mrs. Hunter said. "Because the museum staff will themselves be in period costume, and because they like everyone who comes to the park to immerse themselves in the culture and lifestyle of the early settlers to our area, I strongly encourage all of you to dress the way you would have if we, too, were living in the early to mid eighteen hundreds."

A lot of the girls in the class — with the exception of Rosemary, of course — perked up considerably at this.

Which I *guess* I could understand. Who doesn't love a chance to dress up?

The boys, however, all groaned.

"Does that mean I have to wear knickers?" shouted Stuart Maxwell. "Because I'm not wearing knickers!"

"You don't *have* to do anything, Stuart," Mrs. Hunter said. "I said you're strongly encouraged. And for those of you who do try, there will be fifty points of extra credit."

Everyone began buzzing about the extra credit.

I didn't really *need* any extra credit. . . .

But a personal rule of mine is that *Extra credit is always nice to have, just in case.*

Patrick Day flung his hand in the air.

"Yes, Patrick," Mrs. Hunter said.

"People in those days all had guns," he said. "Will it count as extra credit if I bring my BB gun to school as part of my period costume?"

"No, Patrick," Mrs. Hunter said, "it most definitely will not."

Patrick put his arm down and said, "Dang."

"I'm going to wear a hoopskirt," Cheyenne informed everyone around her. "That's what girls used to wear in those days. My mother knows the owner of a company in New York that rents realistic period costumes, so she'll be able to get one for me."

M and D, Cheyenne's best friends, seemed impressed.

But I saw Erica, who sat near Cheyenne, look a little envious. Like Mrs. Harrington, Erica's mother, who owns a shop downtown where she sells fine collectibles — many of which she makes herself — Erica loves anything to do with dolls, olden times, and dressing up.

I could tell Erica would have dearly loved to wear a rented hoopskirt to school.

What I thought Erica would have loved even more would have been the exhibit of rare collectible Barbies at the Children's Museum. You could dress the Barbies up in hoopskirts. I was almost sure.

"I'm sure a rented costume would be lovely, Cheyenne,"

Mrs. Hunter said. "However, as we've all been learning in class, the pioneers gave up everything they had in order to move out west and make their homesteads here, and couldn't afford store-bought clothes. They made their clothes themselves out of a material called homespun. While I'm not saying all of you who choose to dress in period clothing have to spin your own clothes, it would be more in the spirit of the homesteaders if you used your imagination and assembled your own costumes from clothing you already have in your closets . . . something that might resemble what children who actually lived on Honeypot Prairie might have worn."

I saw Erica perk up at this. She has a pretty big imagination, and *lots* of clothes in her closet.

So do I, actually. Although a lot of them were wadded up at the bottom of my closet. Possibly on top of my Nintendo.

Still. Wearing a costume wasn't going to make a place as boring as Honeypot Prairie any better.

"I'm glad you're all so excited about this," Mrs. Hunter said.

I couldn't understand what Mrs. Hunter was talking about. No one in Room 209 looked excited about going to Honeypot Prairie except Cheyenne.

And she only looked excited about it because of the extra credit she was going to get from the fancy costume she was going to make her mom get her.

"We're going to need that kind of enthusiasm as we finish up our unit on the fascinating life of the early settlers to our area," Mrs. Hunter went on. "I'm also going to need a permission slip signed by your parent or guardian so that you can all come with us to Honeypot Prairie on Friday. Rosemary, the permission slips are sitting on my desk. Will you hand them out?"

Rosemary got up and went to Mrs. Hunter's desk to get the pile of permission slips. When she handed me mine, I was careful to fold it up and put it into the front pocket of my jeans so I wouldn't lose it. There was no way I was going to make the mistake of letting someone else hand it in for me. Or *not* hand it in for me. Not this time.

Honeypot Prairie may be boring and stupid (at least, according to everyone I knew who'd ever been there).

But it was the only field trip I had.

And at least I was finally going to get to ride on a bus.

Rosemary had told me that if you sat toward the back of the bus, over the rear wheels, and the bus went over a pothole or train tracks too fast, you went sailing up into the air.

Because there are no seat belts on the school buses in our town.

This was the most amazing thing I'd ever heard.

"Oh," Mrs. Hunter added. "And one last thing. Because of school budget cuts, we don't have enough money to hire a bus to go to Honeypot Prairie on our own . . ."

All of us froze. I don't know about anyone else, but I immediately began to pray: *Please don't ask our parents to drive us, please don't ask our parents to drive us, please don't ask our parents to drive us.*

I mean, this was my one chance to go somewhere in a school bus! Why would I want to spoil it by going in my own boring car driven by my own boring mom or dad?

". . . so we're going to have to share a bus with another fourth-grade class that will be going the same day we are," Mrs. Hunter went on.

I relaxed. Phew!

Cheyenne's hand shot up into the air.

"Yes, Cheyenne?" Mrs. Hunter definitely sounded tired now.

"With what other school will we be sharing a bus, Mrs. Hunter?" she asked primly.

"Ms. Myers's fourth-grade class," Mrs. Hunter said. "From Walnut Knolls Elementary."

I couldn't believe it:

Walnut Knolls Elementary was my old school, and Ms. Myers was my old teacher.

My first real field trip, and I had to share it — and the bus getting there — with my old class.

Including my ex-best friend, Mary Kay Shiner, who'd ruined my last chance at going on a field trip.

RULE #5

When You're Feeling Bad, the Worst Thing You Can Do Is Inflict Your Bad Mood on Others

This stank more than my mom not letting me buy a cell phone with my own money.

"You don't know for *sure* that Mary Kay is going to try to ruin this field trip for you," Erica said. We were clustered around Lenny Hsu's desk, working on our Honeypot Prairie Group Project that Mrs. Hunter had assigned us. We'd chosen Lenny's desk because it was the tidiest of anyone's in our group. "She and those other girls could have gotten over what happened at Brittany's birthday party by now."

"With my luck?" I shook my head. I felt like crying. I really did. "I don't think so."

Sophie patted me on the shoulder. "Poor Allie."

"I don't get it," Elizabeth Pukowski, who was in our group, said. "What's the big deal about sharing the bus with some girl from Allie's old school?"

"Mary Kay Shiner isn't just *some* girl from Allie's old school," Sophie said.

Then she went on to explain to her about the incident I'd had a few weeks earlier at a birthday party given by Brittany Hauser — who is basically the Cheyenne O'Malley of Walnut Knolls Elementary — at which she and my ex-best friend, Mary Kay Shiner, and some other girls had tried to humiliate me and undermine my self-esteem . . . just because it had gotten around the fourth-grade rumor mill that I had a boyfriend (which is definitely *not* true) and they were jealous.

It had gotten so bad, Uncle Jay's girlfriend, Harmony, had had to drive one hour each way to come rescue me.

Never go to a birthday party given by the most popular girl in your old school just because her mother has rented a limo to take you there. It will NOT turn out well. Rule.

"Seriously?" Elizabeth's eyes widened. "That's *bad*."

"You think that's bad?" asked Patrick Day, who was also in our group. "Check this out." He showed us an extremely large scab that had formed on his elbow. "Road rash from riding my skateboard down the driveway. Way worse than anything that ever happened to Allie at some birthday party."

Sophie, Elizabeth, and Erica let out polite screams. Patrick looked pleased with himself.

"Want to smell it?" he asked.

Sophie said, *"If you don't keep wounds clean, they could become infected, and then might become gangrenous and you could die."*

Erica, always the diplomat, decided to change the subject.

"What about that man?" Erica asked. "The one who was throwing rocks at our windows? Do you think he was Mrs. Hunter's boyfriend?"

"Of course he was," Sophie said. "You could tell he's completely in love with Mrs. Hunter, but she's spurned him."

"What's 'spurned'?" I asked.

"Told him to get lost," Sophie explained, "because she doesn't feel about him the way he feels about her. That's why he was carrying a suitcase. She kicked him out."

My eyes widened. I hadn't thought about the suitcase. Why *had* he been carrying a suitcase?

"I don't think she's spurned him," I said. "I think he was just an old friend, like she said, and he was visiting from somewhere else. And I think she just doesn't want him throwing rocks at our window. That's dangerous. Imagine if the window broke, or if Mrs. Jenkins had seen him doing that." Mrs. Jenkins is the principal, and Mrs. Hunter's boss. "Mrs. Hunter could get in trouble. Maybe even fired. It was really wrong of him to do that."

"I thought it was super romantic," Elizabeth said dreamily. "I hope when I'm old, a guy will come do that to me where I work."

"Can we please stop talking about these very boring things and get back to our report on being female in mid-nineteenth-century America?" Lenny Hsu looked annoyed. "I would like to get a check plus on this project."

"I agree," I said, relieved. "I think we should stop talking about that man. Especially since it was clear from his suitcase that he's going back to where he came from. He's probably never coming back."

"If he loves Mrs. Hunter as much as I think he does," Elizabeth said, "he'll probably come back. But whatever. At least we get to *go* on a field trip. Right? Even if it *is* to someplace boring. And we have to share a bus with some snobby girls. It's better than nothing, right?"

"Right," Sophie agreed. She looked over at me to make sure I wasn't actually crying. Which I wasn't. Yet.

Although the truth was, every time I thought about having to go to Honeypot Prairie — with *Mary Kay Shiner*, of all people — I teared up a little.

And Elizabeth wasn't helping with her *If he loves Mrs. Hunter as much as I think he does, he'll probably come back* remarks. Although don't even ask me why I cared so much about *that*.

"It might be okay, you guys," Erica said, trying to look on the bright side, as usual. "You heard what Mrs. Hunter said. They're going to teach us how to bake bread. And how to shoe a horse! That means there'll be horses there. And you love horses, Allie."

"You can buy bread at the store," I pointed out. "And you don't get to *ride* the horses. You just watch someone else put horseshoes on them." I didn't want to think about how Mary Kay had told me that at the Children's Museum, they'd gotten to play junior fashion stylists and makeup artists, designing Barbies for the next generation using a giant touch-pad screen. That sounded way more fun than anything I'd heard so far about what Honeypot Prairie had to offer. "The rest of the time we'll be crammed into a dinky one-room schoolhouse learning about how bad things were in olden times."

With Mary Kay Shiner . . . and Brittany Hauser! And Cheyenne O'Malley! *At the same time!*

"Like we don't already know how bad things were in olden times," I went on. "We practically live in olden times ourselves! At least, those of us who don't have cell phones do."

"Yeah," Elizabeth said, shaking her head at me sympathetically. "You do."

That's when I realized *she* had a cell phone.

Lenny Hsu had one, too! I saw him tapping away at it beneath his desk, bored from all our girl talk.

And even though the whole rest of the day, I tried hard to be like Erica and look on the bright side and not bring everyone down into the dumps with me — *When you're feeling bad, the worst thing you can do is inflict your bad mood on others* — all I could think about was how horrible my life was going lately. My friends kept assuring me that no matter what, they'd stick by me, and not let Mary Kay and those other girls be mean to me on Friday.

Still, I couldn't shake the feeling that my first field trip ever was going to be totally spoiled by a lot of mean girls from my past.

I was still fuming about that — and Mrs. Hunter's

maybe boyfriend — when I got home from school at the end of the day and saw a big red van parked in our driveway.

A+ ROOFERS, it said in yellow on the side.

"But that isn't what you said just eight months ago," my dad was saying to a man holding a clipboard who was standing in the hallway outside my brother Mark's bedroom. "When you inspected the roof before we bought this house, you said it was fine."

"Well," the man said, scratching beneath his hard hat. "That may have been true eight months ago. But we've had a lot of snow and rain since then. You've got yourself an old house with an old roof with a lot of eaves and gables. If you want to fix the leaks and kill the dry rot going on inside your walls, you're going to have to replace a lot of shingles."

I wasn't sure. But this sounded like a rule to me.

"Mom," Mark said because he was standing right there between my mom and dad, "can I go out onto the roof with Mr. Johnson to help replace the shingles?"

"No," Mom said.

"Can I go inside the hole in the wall in Mark's closet?" Kevin, who was standing next to Mark, asked.

"No," Mom said.

"Then can I wear your hard hat, Mr. Johnson?" Kevin asked, cocking his head to one side like Marvin when he wants a dog biscuit. When Mark and I had caught Kevin trying this look out in front of the mirror, Kevin had told us it was his "cute" look, and that whenever he used it, people gave him whatever he wanted. We'd laughed at him for a long time over that one. "Please?"

"Tell you what," Mr. Johnson said, looking down at Kevin with a big smile on his craggy face. "If your parents accept my estimate and hire me to do the job, I'll bring you a hard hat of your very own."

"Gee, Mr. Johnson," Kevin said. "That'd be great."

I couldn't believe it.

Kevin's "cute" look actually worked!

It wasn't fair. Kevin *always* gets what he wants (well, except velvet pants).

But do *I* ever get what I want?

No!

After carefully sticking my permission slip under a magnet on the refrigerator door for my mom and dad to sign (I wasn't letting anything bad happen to this one, even if it was only to go to Honeypot Prairie and not anywhere good), I went into my room and shut my door (careful not to slam it or I'd have gotten in trouble. *No slamming doors* is a rule in our house).

What was even the point? I wondered with a sigh, going to stretch out on my bed. Just like the children of the pioneers, I'd worked very hard (earning thirty-six whole dollars), and for what? My crops to be ruined by swarms of locusts?

Now my big chance to finally go on a field trip had come along, and my ex-best friend had to come back to haunt me.

I swear, I sort of *felt* like the kid of an early settler. We'd learned in class that vacations were invented because this was when the children of the pioneers were needed on the farm . . . to help their parents in the fields during planting time. In some states, Mrs. Hunter had told us, they've been thinking of getting rid of summer vacations because parents have a hard time finding child care for their kids while they're at work during the summer months. No one is allowed to hire kids to work on farms anymore, due to child labor laws.

I couldn't believe the unfairness of this! No more summer breaks? That meant no more swimming, no more camp, no more lying around in the backyard, daydreaming and looking for ants to help back to their anthill!

Still, it must have been horrible in olden times to get out of school for vacation just to have to go work in a field.

And the kids in those days couldn't even buy cell phones with the money they earned (if their parents even gave them an allowance) because cell phones hadn't been invented yet!

Being the kid of an early settler stank.

A lot like being Allie Finkle.

RULE #6

You Should Never Read Other People's Private Correspondence

Mr. Johnson gave Kevin a hard hat. That's because his company won the estimate to work on our new roof.

I'd have thought my parents would have been excited about this, since they had bought an old house on purpose to have the fun of fixing it up.

But all my dad did was go around muttering, "Six thousand dollars," under his breath.

Mom and Dad might have owed the roofing man six thousand dollars, but *I* was the one who was really suffering. I had to go on a field trip to the most boring place in the entire world, and on the same bus as my ex-best friend, who had accidentally on purpose ruined my last field trip!

Not only that, but I had to walk my little brother to and from school every day, while he was wearing a *hard hat*.

It was totally embarrassing!

Not that my friends were embarrassed. They thought it was cute, as usual.

But Kevin's embarrassing affection for his new hard hat and my having to go on a field trip to a totally boring place with my ex-best friend, Mary Kay Shiner, weren't the only things that were upsetting me.

Even the fact that my mom still wouldn't budge on the cell phone issue, despite how responsible I'd been trying to be (and okay, I still hadn't found my Nintendo, even though I'd searched through my entire closet while looking for something 1850-ish to wear on Friday), wasn't bugging me as much as this other thing.

No, what was *really* bothering me was what had happened while I'd been presenting our group project to the class the day before our field trip to Honeypot Prairie.

I had been standing in front of Room 209 (because my group had elected me spokesperson. Which was all right, because I am going to be a veterinarian slash actress when

I grow up, so I don't mind speaking in front of crowds. I mean, it's a *little* scary, having so many pairs of eyes on you. But I just tell myself one of my favorite rules: *It's all good practice for when you're famous)*, talking about life in the 1850s.

"Being a woman in eighteen fifties America was very hard," I was saying. "Basically, the only jobs you could have if you were a woman back then were a laundress, a seamstress, a maid, a nanny, a factory worker, or a teacher or nurse . . . *if* you were lucky enough to be accepted to one of the few colleges that let women go to them, which there weren't many of back then. You couldn't be anything else, especially if you were African-American or Native American or Asian-American. For instance, you couldn't be a veterinarian. You could be an actress, but that would scandalize your family and they would pretend not to know you. You couldn't be a lawyer or a doctor or a scientist or a railroad engineer or a writer (unless you wrote under an anonymous name), and you couldn't be a politician because women weren't even allowed to vote. So, basically, being a woman in olden times was very, very bad."

It was right then that there was a knock on the classroom door and Mrs. Wright, the administrative assistant from Mrs. Jenkins's office, came in.

And she was carrying the biggest bouquet of red roses I had ever seen. They were so big, you could barely even see Mrs. Wright's head.

"Mrs. Hunter," Mrs. Wright said, smiling really big from behind the roses. "These just arrived for you. I thought I'd better bring them right up because . . . well, there isn't really room for them in the office."

She set them in their crystal vase on the stool next to where I was standing and left, still smiling.

We all stared at the bouquet. So did Mrs. Hunter, from her desk where she was still sitting in the back of the room, her mouth open just a little bit in astonishment.

Cheyenne was the first one to say anything, as usual.

"Mrs. Hunter," she said, her hand flying into the air. "Aren't you going to see who they're from?"

"Yes, I am," Mrs. Hunter said. She'd started to turn a little pink. "I'm very sorry for the interruption, class."

Mrs. Hunter got up from her seat and hurried to the

front of the room, her high heels making tippity-tap sounds on the floor. Then she picked up the little white envelope that was sitting tucked inside the roses. It seemed to take her a long time to get the envelope open.

All of us watched in total silence. I looked over at Caroline and Erica and Sophie, like, *Can you believe this?*

But they just looked back at me like, *Whoa. No.* So did everyone else in the class . . .

. . . except Cheyenne, who was giggling and whispering excitedly with M and D.

What did Cheyenne know that we didn't?

Everything, apparently. Well, Cheyenne thinks she knows everything, anyway.

I was sure when *I* got a cell phone, I'd know everything, too.

I was standing next to the huge bouquet, which, sitting on the stool, was as tall as me. I couldn't believe how much those roses smelled. Also, how many of them there were. It was like being inside a rose garden. Or a beauty pageant.

Mrs. Hunter had finally gotten the envelope open and was reading what the scribbly writing said on the tiny card that had come inside it. She was standing so close to me that I couldn't help stealing a little glance at the card as well. I didn't *mean* to look.

But it was right there in front of me!

And even though I know it's a rule that *You should never read other people's private correspondence*, it was like my eyes were just glued to that card. I couldn't pull them away! I was just so curious about who had sent Mrs. Hunter flowers in the middle of a school day.

Even though I sort of already knew. It had to be the man with the suitcase, the one who had thrown rocks at our windows.

But unfortunately, I couldn't tell what he'd said on the card. It just looked like a big old bunch of scribbles to me (I've never been very good at reading cursive written by grown-ups).

The only word I could really read was the signature.

David.

David? Was David the name of Mrs. Hunter's old friend?

"Well," Mrs. Hunter said finally, looking up from

the card. She had a big smile on her face. Whoever David was and whatever he had said in his card, Mrs. Hunter definitely liked it. "I apologize for the disturbance, class. Excellent job, Allie." She patted me on the back. For a second I couldn't figure out why. Then I remembered that I'd just finished my presentation. "Check plus plus!"

Well, I thought, *at least Lenny will be happy.*

Then Mrs. Hunter picked up the giant vase of roses, staggered back to her desk with it, and called for the next group to give their presentation.

Just like that! Like nothing had happened at all!

Of course at recess, everyone came up to me and asked what the card had said.

And I had to admit to them that I didn't know! Because I hadn't been able to read the writing on it. Except for the name: David.

"He asked her to marry him," Cheyenne said with her usual know-it-all-ness. "He *had* to have."

"That's so dorky." I couldn't believe her. She thinks she knows everything! "Who would send flowers asking someone to marry them *at their job?* That's not romantic. Mrs. Hunter would never marry a guy like that."

Although the truth was, now that Cheyenne mentioned it, I realized the words on the card *could* have said *Would you marry me? Love, David.*

But they could also have said a lot of other things! Such as, *Thanks for letting me stay at your apartment while I was in town visiting. I had a very nice time. You are an excellent hostess. Sincerely yours, David.*

They could very easily have said that. That would be a proper thing to say to an old friend who had let you stay on her foldout couch.

Cheyenne rolled her eyes. "You're such an immature baby, Allie. It was that same man with the suitcase who threw rocks at our window the other day. Her old friend. Mrs. Hunter obviously reconnected with an old flame, and he can't stand to be away from her even for a second because he's so very much in love with her. So he asked her to marry him. *I* think it's very romantic."

Joey Fields, who'd been hanging around listening to our conversation, as he often does at recess because none of the boys will play with him because he's so weird and barks all the time, said, looking directly at me, "I plan on proposing to the woman I love *exactly* the same way."

I rolled my eyes and suggested we go play queens. Joey never follows us into the bushes because he's afraid of thorns.

Later that day, when we were sitting on the bed at Erica's house after school, I couldn't help saying, "I just don't like it."

"Why not?" Erica cried, looking disappointed as she stood in front of her full-length mirror.

"Not your outfit," I said quickly. "Mrs. Hunter and this David guy."

"What don't you like?" Caroline asked.

"If they get married," I said, "he's going to make her move to wherever he lives out of town."

"Why would he do that?" Sophie asked. "He could move here to live with Mrs. Hunter."

"We don't even know they're getting married," Caroline said. "Cheyenne just made that up. You know how she is."

But I knew that Cheyenne was right. Because Mrs. Hunter getting married and moving away was the worst thing that could happen.

And lately hadn't all the worst things that *could* happen to me happened?

"We're all going into fifth grade next year, anyway," Caroline said. "So what does it even matter?"

"But Mrs. Hunter might teach fifth grade next year," I said.

"What?" everyone cried, looking at me.

Also, "Where did you hear that?" they asked.

And, "I never heard Mrs. Hunter was going to be teaching fifth grade next year."

"Well," I said slowly. "I don't know where I heard that."

I didn't want to admit that I had just made this up because I liked Mrs. Hunter so much that I couldn't bear the thought of having some other teacher next year.

Kind of the way Cheyenne had made it up about Mrs. Hunter and David getting married.

"I'm just saying it *could* happen," I said. "Teachers switch grades sometimes, if they really, really like their students."

Especially if it's a student who is as much a joy to have around the classroom as I am.

"But if she marries this David guy and he makes her move away to wherever he lives, it definitely won't happen," I added.

"I like Mrs. Hunter," Caroline said. "But I wouldn't mind having someone new for fifth grade."

I couldn't believe Caroline would say this. I wanted Mrs. Hunter to be my teacher *forever!*

"I don't think Mrs. Hunter is the kind of person who would do something just because a man asked her to," Sophie said. "I mean, unless David is a doctor for very poor people in some underdeveloped country without running water, and he asked her to go there with him to help teach the little orphans while he heals the sick. Then I could see her doing it."

My mom says Sophie's parents let Sophie watch way too much unsupervised TV.

"I don't think Mrs. Hunter would want her little boy to be in some country without running water, around very sick people," Erica said. "Anyway, what do you think? Do you think I look like a girl from the eighteen fifties?"

We all looked at the outfit she was wearing.

"Totally," I said.

Because one of my rules is that *It's always better to lie if that lie makes someone feel better.*

"Definitely," Caroline said.

"Well," Sophie said. "Not really."

Caroline and I shot Sophie a look. The look said *What's wrong with you?*

Because Erica had been freaking out all week about putting together her extra-credit period costume to Honeypot Prairie.

Now we were sitting in her bedroom playing fashion stylists (unfortunately, without the help of a giant touch-pad screen like they had at the Barbie exhibit at the Children's Museum), trying to find the perfect thing that a girl from 1850s America might wear, and we'd finally kind of come up with something we all had in our closets.

But Sophie had ruined it.

"I'm sorry," Sophie said. "But no girl in the eighteen fifties would have worn jeans and a flannel shirt. That's how *boys* dressed. Girls all had to wear long dresses. It was against the law for them to do anything else, like Allie said in her presentation."

"Well," I said. "Mrs. Hunter just said we had to *try*. She didn't say we had to do it exactly perfect."

"Right," Caroline said. "And we can't help it if things back in the eighteen fifties were totally unfair. I mean, the women had to work just as hard as the men — but they had to do it all in a long dress with no right to vote and with half the pay, or sometimes no pay."

"This is so dumb," Sophie said in frustration. "I don't know why we're even trying. Those girls from Walnut Knolls — not to mention Cheyenne — are going to look *way* better than we do no matter what we wear, anyway. At least based on everything Allie said about that birthday party!"

Sometimes I wished I hadn't complained quite so much as I had about what had happened at Brittany's birthday party. A good rule is *If you went somewhere and had a terrible time, maybe tone it down a little when you're describing it to people later, or they might blow it out of proportion, and then it could come back to haunt you.*

"But the costume thing is for extra credit," I pointed out. "And besides, Cheyenne's cheating. Mrs. Hunter said the costumes have to be homemade."

"Cheyenne isn't *still* going to do that," Erica said. "I mean, not after Mrs. Hunter said not to."

We all just looked at Erica.

"Okay," Erica said, seeing our reflections in her mirror. "You guys can think I'm dumb, but I refuse to believe it. Even *Cheyenne* wouldn't do something like that after Mrs. Hunter came right out and told us not to."

We looked at her some more. Then Erica laughed.

"Oh, all *right*," she said. "You're probably right. And I guess I *do* look totally modern in this."

"What are you troglodytes doing?" a voice from the doorway asked.

64

RULE #7

It's Very Rude to Call Someone a Troglodyte

"Please stop calling us that, Missy," Erica said. "My friends are not troglodytes."

It makes Erica very upset that her sister calls us troglodytes, but it doesn't really bother me since none of us lives in a cave (although the fact that only one of us has a cell phone does make us a bit old-fashioned), and that's the definition of "troglodyte," which we'd once looked up — an old-fashioned hermit who lives in a cave.

Although *It's very rude to call someone a troglodyte*. That's a rule.

"Whatever you say, trog," Missy said. "Why are you wearing one of John's flannel shirts?"

"If you must know," Erica said stiffly, "it's because we're

going to Honeypot Prairie tomorrow, and we're trying to come up with some homemade period costumes so we can get extra credit —"

"And *that's* what you came up with?" Missy sneered through her headgear. "Jeans and one of your brother's shirts? Why don't you come to me about these things, trog? I've *been* to Honeypot Prairie, you know. It's completely boring, but at least I know of a great homemade period costume that won't make you look like a trog."

We all stared at Erica's sister. Missy is a very, very talented gymnast.

But as a teenager, she can also be a bit moody. Also, somewhat devious.

"Like what?" Caroline asked suspiciously.

Missy shook her head at us. "It's called a nightgown. With one of Mom's aprons over it. Right? Because nightgowns are like long dresses. And with an apron over one, you look exactly like one of those prairie ladies." Missy sighed. "What would you trogs do without me? I honestly don't know."

Then she did a back handspring out of Erica's room and into the hallway.

"I'm sorry." Erica looked at all of us with tears in her eyes after her sister was gone. "I don't know why she's so mean. My mom says it's her hormones and we should just be patient. But honestly, I don't know if I —"

"Wait," Caroline said. "Her idea is sort of genius."

"A *nightgown*?" Sophie laughed. "*You can't wear a nightgown to school.* There are boys there. You can't wear a nightgown in front of boys. That's just wrong."

Erica flushed. "Sophie's right. I could never wear a nightgown to school."

"But the apron covers everything up," I said, agreeing with Caroline that the idea was kind of genius. "It's not like anyone can see anything, or even tell it's a nightgown."

"It's better than anything else we've come up with," Caroline said mournfully. "But I don't even own a nightgown. All I have are pj's."

"You can borrow one of mine," I said. "My grandma

sends me a flannel Lanz of Salzburg nightgown every year for my birthday and Christmas." Not that this was what I had ever asked for. Grandma was just afraid I might catch a cold from a draft, because this was very common when she was a girl, and now we live in such an old house.

"My mom doesn't have any aprons," Sophie said.

"My mom has tons," Erica said. "You can each borrow one."

"I can't believe we're going to wear nightgowns to school," Sophie said, shaking her head in disbelief.

"If we wear leggings under them," I said, "and T-shirts, it won't be any different than regular clothes. So who cares?"

Erica took us downstairs to the kitchen, where her mom keeps all her aprons. She did have a ton, and most of them did look pretty old-timey. After calling Mrs. Harrington at her shop to make sure it was okay, we picked out the ones we liked most.

Then I went home to hunt through my closet for nightgowns that would look the most 1850s. I didn't ask if Caroline wanted to come with me to choose one (Sophie

and Erica both said they had their own nightgowns),
on account of my house being a complete disaster area.
That's because Mr. Johnson and all his roofing guys
were there, stomping around on the roof, ripping off shingles. There were ladders leaning up against the house, and
Kevin and Mark were running around the front yard, trying to "help."

Only I don't know how much "help" they were being.

"Allie," Kevin said to me, wearing his hard hat, which
was way too big for his head, all wobbly. "Don't even
bother asking Mom and Dad if you can go up on the roof.
Because they just made that a new rule: *No Finkle kid can go
on the roof.*"

"Well, I have no desire to go on the roof," I said. "So
that's not going to be a problem."

I went inside and upstairs to my room and started sort-
ing through my nightgowns. I tried to think what I'd want
to be seen in at school . . . and what I wouldn't mind Mary
Kay and those guys seeing me in.

It was kind of a hard decision. Especially with all the
stomping coming from up on the roof. And my brain kind

of distracted by the whole thing with Mrs. Hunter and her boyfriend, which was still bothering me, at least a little.

I knew from the pictures we'd seen that girls' dresses from those days wouldn't be too fancy, like lacy and stuff, because all the early settlers were very poor, and couldn't afford lace, which was expensive back in those days.

An early settler, for instance, wouldn't have been able to call to order a pizza for dinner when she was tired out from a long day of going to school and finding out her teacher might be getting married.

First of all because there were no phones (much less cell phones) back in the 1850s.

And second of all because there was no such thing as pizza deliverymen (or even pizza) back then. The early settlers had to make all their own food. From scratch.

Teachers couldn't even have *had* big bunches of roses delivered to them at school from their boyfriends back in those days. Because there were no flower deliverymen. Or delivery vans.

The kids of early settlers were kind of lucky in *that* way.

I had finally settled on a red nightgown with blue stripes and yellow flowers on it for me, and a blue nightgown with red stripes and white flowers on it for Caroline, when I realized something was . . . missing.

And it wasn't the cell phone I, unlike the early settlers, had enough money to buy, but wasn't allowed to have, either.

"Mewsie?" I said, looking around my room.

It isn't unusual for my cat, Mewsie, not to come right away when I call. Even though he's an indoor cat (so far. He'd really, really like to go outside, but I made a rule that he wasn't allowed to, and that everyone in my family had to be very careful not to let him outside, because he could be hit by a car or get lost), he sometimes wanders very far away from my room, and curls up and falls asleep in weird places, and doesn't hear me when I call him.

But this time, when I went to look for him in all of the usual places, like on top of my mom's shoes in her closet or in the planter in the living room, Mewsie was nowhere to be found.

Suddenly, all of the bad things that had happened to me lately — like being called irresponsible and not being allowed to get the cell phone I'd always wanted, or that I was going to have to ride the bus to Honeypot Prairie with my ex-best friend, Mary Kay, or that my favorite teacher might be moving away and getting married — seemed not to matter at all anymore.

The truth is, nothing else matters when you realize you might have lost the one thing you care about more than anything else in the whole world.

RULE #8

Nothing Else Matters When
You've Lost the One Thing You Care
About More Than Anything Else
in the Whole World

"Mom!"

I barged into the dining room, where Mom and Dad seemed to be having a serious talk. I could tell it was serious because Dad was sitting down with his head in his hands saying, "Six thousand dollars!" while Mom was standing over him saying everything was going to be all right.

"Not now, Allie," Mom said. "Your father and I are talking."

"But, Mom," I yelled. *"Mewsie's gone!"*

"Allie," Dad said to his lap, "I have a really bad headache, and you are not making it any better with all that yelling."

"But he's gone!" I couldn't believe they weren't seeing how serious the situation was. I ran around the dining room table. "I can't find him anywhere! I think he must have gotten outside. Maybe Mr. Johnson or some of his roofing guys let him out. Didn't you tell them the *rule*?"

"Of course we did," Mom said. "Calm down, Allie. I'm sure Mewsie is around here somewhere."

"He isn't," I cried. "I've looked everywhere! He has to have gotten outside!"

"Well," Dad said, lifting his head from his hands. "Go outside and look for him, then."

I couldn't understand how they could be so calm when the life of my cat could possibly be at stake. Didn't they know the things that could happen to a cat who had gotten outside for the first time?

He could get confused and wander into some other neighborhood and never find his way home again.

He could crawl into the engine of someone's parked

74

car and then when the person got in and started the engine to drive away, the cat could get sucked up inside the motor.

Or he could climb a tree and accidentally go too far and get stuck in the upper branches and get scared and not be able to crawl down again, then slowly starve to death.

Or someone could be walking along and see him sitting on the sidewalk and think, *What a beautiful cat* (because of course Mewsie is the most beautiful cat in the whole world), and just decide to pick him up and take him home to live with them, not even caring that he has a microchip embedded in his neck that says he belongs to me, Allie Finkle.

And Mewsie, because he is very sweet and trusting and, unlike the children of the early settlers and myself, has never known hardship, would never scratch or bite someone who picked him up from the sidewalk.

"Don't you understand?" I yelled. By now I was crying. "We have to call the police!"

"We are not calling the police," Mom said, "because you can't find your cat, Allie. What's the matter with you?"

"E-everything's horrible!" I cried.

"Oh?" Dad said. "Is A-Plus charging you six thousand dollars to reshingle your roof, too?"

"Thomas!" Mom said, giving Dad a disapproving look.

"What's going on?" Mark asked. I guess he'd heard all the yelling and come inside to find out what was going on. "What's wrong with Allie?"

"Nothing's wrong with Allie." Mom walked over to wipe off some of my tears with the bottom of her shirt. "She can't find her cat."

"Want me to help look for him?" Mark asked. "I'm exceptional at finding things. When the newts in my class escaped from their terrarium when Casey Giarardi forgot to put the lid back on when he cleaned it, I'm the one who found them in the heating duct."

"Mewsie's not a newt!" I yelled at him.

"Well, when Mewsie went missing last time," he said, "it was my idea to look in the dryer."

"I already looked in the dryer," I said. I buried my face in Mom's soft stomach. Her mom smell was comforting.

Though not enough to calm me down completely. "He isn't in the dryer."

It's amazing how quickly life can go from being just a little bit bad to a total disaster. Like in the blink of an eye.

This was probably how the children of the early settlers felt. Like when bugs would get into the seed corn, and they would think, *Oh, well, at least there's the sugar beets*. Then a frost would kill all the sugar beets.

Or when you think you have enough money to buy a cell phone, your parents could make some new rule like, *Oh, no, you can't have a cell phone until you're in the sixth grade, even if you buy it with your own money*.

Or you could have the best teacher in the world, and some man you don't even know could come along and steal her away.

Proving none of us has any idea how truly awful things can get.

That's what I was telling myself as I was staggering around the front yard in the dark a few hours later, my eyes all red-rimmed with tears, going, "Mewsie! Mewsie! Here, kitty, kitty!" in a voice that was hoarse from having called the same thing over and over again, for so long and so loud that Erica and her big brother, John, and even her sister, Missy, had heard me and come out of their house next door to help me to look.

That's what we were all doing when Uncle Jay drove up.

"Hi, Allie," he said, getting out of the driver's side of his beat-up car that has a light-up Pizza Express sign screwed to the roof. His girlfriend, Harmony, who has long, shiny black hair, got out of the passenger side. They were both carrying pizza boxes.

"Heard the Finkle family is having kind of a tough week," Harmony said, smiling at me.

I had no idea what she was talking about. Nothing bad had happened to the *rest* of my family, except that my parents had to buy a new roof because the old one leaked. Who even cared about that? *I* was the one who was having a tough week. On top of everything else that had gone wrong, like with the cell phone and the field trip to stupid

Honeypot Prairie and Mary Kay and my wonderful teacher getting stolen away by some stranger, which I barely even cared about anymore, my cat was missing. A feline life was at stake!

And my family didn't even care.

Except that I supposed losing my cat was going to make Mom and Dad think I was even *less* responsible now. Like it was *my* fault the roofing men hadn't obeyed the rule, and left the door open.

I *knew* there was something wrong with that Mr. Johnson. Anyone who would fall for Kevin's cute face is not to be trusted.

"Come on, Allie, cheer up," Uncle Jay said. "I'm sure Mewsie's just gone on a walkabout."

Erica and her brother and sister had waved good-night to me from the yard, wishing me luck. I barely noticed. I was busy following Uncle Jay and Harmony up onto the front porch.

"What's a walkabout?" I asked.

"It's when someone feels the need to break away from the daily grind," Uncle Jay said, "in the hope of eventually finding his spiritual path. So he takes off for a while to have some new adventures."

Tears filled my eyes again.

"But I don't *want* Mewsie to take off for a while to have some new adventures," I said with a wail.

"Oh, Allie," Harmony said, wrapping an arm around my shoulders. "I'm sure Mewsie's fine. Jay didn't mean it like that."

"Yes, I did," Uncle Jay said. "That's the thing with a walkabout, Allie. Fighting it doesn't do anybody any good."

I stared at Uncle Jay like he was crazy. So did Harmony.

"That's nuts," I cried. "Mewsie's not seeking his spiritual path. He's a cat!"

"Well," Uncle Jay said. "I'm just saying. Walkabouts happen. It's like . . . well, one of your rules. You just have to accept it."

I reached up to dry my eyes with the sleeve of my windbreaker.

"It is *not* a rule! I'm not just going to *accept* that Mewsie has gone on a walkabout," I said, my hoarse voice breaking. "I'm going to stay out here all night, calling for him, if I have to. And if he doesn't come home tonight, I'm going to make flyers tomorrow with a picture of him and a description, and hang them all over the neighborhood, asking for people's help looking for him. And I'm going to call the animal shelter every single day to see if anyone has brought him in. And I'm going to make Mom hold up one of the flyers on her TV show, even if it is only on a local station. And I'm *never* going to stop looking for him, ever —"

"Hey, Allie!"

The glass storm door opened, and Mark stood there, panting like he'd just run very fast from some faraway place.

"What?" I asked him, still crying. "Mark, I'm having a very important conversation right now."

"Kevin and I found Mewsie," he said.

My heart heaved. *"Where?"*

"You'll never believe it," he said. "Follow me."

He started thumping up the stairs. I thumped after him, my pulse racing almost as fast as my feet. *You'll never believe it.*

What did *that* mean? Was Mewsie all right? Did this mean he *hadn't* gone on a walkabout?

If Mewsie was all right, I told myself as I followed Mark, I would do everything within my power to become a more responsible person. I would try to accept the fact that we were going to Honeypot Prairie on our field trip tomorrow and not somewhere *good* like the Children's Museum, and I would stop complaining about that (in my head).

I would try to accept the fact that Mrs. Hunter *might* not be willing to switch from teaching fourth grade to fifth grade just for me. And that she might want to marry someone someday, and move away.

If Mewsie was all right, I would not only become more responsible about these things but I would stop complaining about my parents refusing to let me have a cell phone, or even buy one with my own money. I wouldn't even complain anymore (in my head) about stupid Mary Kay Shiner.

Who cares about a cell phone, or riding on a bus with my ex-best friend, anyway?

Not me.

None of those things mattered.

All that matters are the people — and pets — you love.

That was probably the number one rule of all.

I just had to remember that.

Mark swerved around the corner at the top of the stairs, disappearing into his bedroom. I followed him . . . then skidded to a stop.

RULE #9

Make Sure Your Little Brothers Don't Do Stupid Things

Kevin was sitting on the floor of Mark's closet, picking what appeared to be mushrooms off his shirt. He was covered in dust and grime and . . . snail shells.

"You went into the wall!" I accused him.

Mark and Kevin both shushed me.

"Not so loud," Mark said. "Do you want Mom and Dad to find out? They'll kill us. Or take away our Nintendos, at least."

"But . . ." I couldn't believe it. We weren't allowed to go into the wall. Dad had said so. It was a rule. "It's dangerous in there. You could have gotten stuck. Or fallen through the dry rot. Or made the entire house collapse on us!"

Kevin looked at me blankly. "Allie," he said, "I wore my hard hat."

"I wanted to go," Mark said. "But I couldn't fit. So I shined Dad's flashlight on Kevin while he went. And guess what we found."

"I don't care." I was mad. As a big sister, it's my responsibility to make sure my little brothers don't do stupid things, like crawl into holes in the walls of their closets that my parents had to put there to check on dry rot and leaks. "You could have been killed!"

"We found Mewsie," Kevin said.

"You did?" I looked quickly around Mark's room, my heart speeding up again. "Where? Where is he?"

Mark pointed with the flashlight at the dark hole out of which Kevin had just crawled. "In there."

All the spit in my mouth dried up.

"Mewsie is . . . *in the wall?*"

Kevin nodded eagerly. "Way in the back," he said. "All curled up in the corner."

"Look," Mark said, switching the flashlight on. "You can see him."

85

I grabbed the flashlight.

"Wait," Kevin said. "Wear this."

I didn't want to, but I felt like I had to, for safety's sake. I put on his hard hat. Then I ducked my head and shoulders into the hole. I could wiggle in pretty far . . .

. . . even though it was super dark and creepy in there, and there were all those mushrooms and snails and probably spiders, too.

I didn't care, though. That's how much I wanted to find my cat.

"Where?" I demanded from inside the woodsy-smelling hole. "I don't see him." I could see deep into the inner caverns of the interior of our house . . . all beams and two-by-fours, under what the roofing man would have called the eaves. . . .

And then I heard it. A tiny *Mrowr?* that is the sleepy sound with which Mewsie greets me every time I walk into a room and wake him up.

And my flashlight beam fell on two bright, glowing dots . . . cat's eyes. And a tiny gray and black striped body, curled up in a dark corner beneath an eave, all snug and warm and happy as a clam.

"Mewsie!" I cried. "Oh, Mewsie!"

I was so happy and relieved, I didn't care that I too was probably getting dry rot and snail all over me. Mewsie was alive! And safe! He hadn't gone on a walkabout.

Okay, he was in the wall.

But he wasn't outside, getting sucked into someone's car engine or being catnapped.

"Mewsie," I called. "Here, kitty!"

"He won't come," I heard Mark say behind me. "We already tried calling him. He likes it in there."

"Allie!"

Suddenly, my ankles were seized, and I was dragged out from inside the wall. I took off Kevin's hard hat and found myself blinking up at Uncle Jay.

"What are you doing in there?" he asked in disbelief.

"Mewsie's in the wall," I said. "He's been there this whole time. He didn't go on a walkabout."

"Oh." Uncle Jay scratched his chin. "Well, that's good.

87

I guess. Listen, your mom wants you to go set the table for dinner. And you better wash your hands first. And, uh, comb your hair."

I stared at him like he was crazy.

"I can't come to dinner," I said. "I have to get Mewsie out of the wall."

"Why?" Uncle Jay looked confused. "He's fine."

"But he can't stay inside the wall!" I couldn't believe this. Was I the only person in my entire family who understood the proper care of pets? "It isn't safe. What if the roofing people come back? They could knock him down into a hole or something. And then he'll get trapped, and we won't be able to get him out. And he'll be stuck there forever and turn into a cat skeleton."

Uncle Jay shook his head.

"Allie," he said. "He's a cat. He's not going to fall down any holes."

How could Uncle Jay not understand this?

"He already went into a hole," I pointed out to him. "The one in Mark's wall. What if there are *more* holes in there?" I asked. "And he finds them and goes in them, deeper and deeper inside the house, until —"

"Until what?" Uncle Jay asked. "He ends up where? Narnia?"

I just stared at Uncle Jay. Of course Mewsie wasn't going to end up in Narnia. There is no such place. Because it's made up. I'm pretty sure.

And if there *were* such a place, I highly doubt you could get to it through a hole in Mark's wall. At least, I hadn't seen any talking mice or ice queens while I'd been in there.

"No," I said. "But —"

"Look," Uncle Jay said. "Just put some cat treats down on the floor and ignore him. He'll come out when he gets hungry. And then when he does, we'll close Mark's closet door and Mewsie won't be able to go in there again. End of story."

This sounded like the stupidest plan ever.

Or maybe the smartest. I couldn't decide.

But since the only other plan I could think of was to

sit in front of the hole in Mark's closet wall, crying and begging Mewsie to come out, I decided to go with Uncle Jay's plan. Since the truth was, I was pretty hungry for dinner. And I didn't think my plan was going to work.

I went into my room and got the little bag of cat treats that Santa had given to Mewsie in his Christmas stocking (not that I believe in Santa. Necessarily).

Then, after shaking the bag a few times outside the hole, and calling to Mewsie (but of course, he didn't budge. He liked it there in Narnia too much. Only it wasn't really Narnia, of course), I left a little pile of the treats on Mark's bedroom floor.

Then I washed my hands and combed my hair and went down to set the table for dinner, which was delicious pizza from Pizza Express (or at least, the pizza was delicious after I lifted up the cheese and scraped off all the tomato sauce, which I have to do because one of my rules is *Never eat anything red*).

What else could I do? At least I knew where Mewsie was.

Then, as soon as dinner was over, after helping put the dishes in the dishwasher, I ran back upstairs . . .

. . . just in time to catch Mewsie, having come out to eat the *entire* pile of cat treats (he's such a pig sometimes, for a cat), dart back inside the hole.

"Nooooo!" I yelled, lunging after him.

But it was too late.

"Mrowr?" he said to me from deep inside the hole in a completely cheerful way, like he thought the whole thing was a wonderful game.

"Mewsie," I called into the hole. "Come out of there!"

But he wouldn't.

Uncle Jay was right: There was nothing I could do.

My cat was on a walkabout.

And I just had to wait until his spiritual quest was over, and he was ready to come home.

RULE #10

It's Rude to Tell Someone They Look Like a French Poodle. Unless They Are, in Fact, a French Poodle

I don't think I'd ever been in as bad a mood as I was on the day of my first field trip ever.

"Absolutely not," Mom said when I asked if I could just stay home.

"But, Mom, you don't understand," I pleaded with her. "Mewsie —"

"— is *fine*," Mom said. "We know exactly where he is. He's completely safe, and nothing is going to happen to him."

Mom was so, so wrong.

"But what if —"

"Allie," Mom said. "You've been wanting to go on a field trip your entire life. Now is your big chance. And you're trying to get out of it? What's wrong with you?"

What was wrong with me was that my cat was on a walkabout, and I was really worried. I was going to be so far away — all the way at stupid, boring Honeypot Prairie — with no cell phone, and no way to reach me if anything happened.

But my mom made me turn around and march back to my room and get dressed. I was going to Honeypot Prairie whether I liked it or not.

As it happened, I did *not* like it.

"Ha," Kevin said when he saw me in my nightgown and apron. "You look funny."

"Oh," I said, staring pointedly at his hard hat. "And you look real normal."

"Workmen wear these," he informed me.

"Yeah," I said, showing him my fist. "Well, you'll be wearing this if you don't shut up."

"Allie!" Mom said, shocked. "You know we do not condone violence in this family."

It was fine for her. *She* hadn't been up all night, worrying about *her* cat, who was shivering in the cold and dark (and okay, maybe it wasn't cold inside the wall. It was actually pretty warm, which was why Mewsie liked it, and wouldn't come out. So Mewsie hadn't actually been shivering at all).

But whatever.

There were probably mice in there, too. Which was another reason Mewsie liked it.

Great! My sweet, adorable cat was in the wall, catching and eating dangerous, disease-carrying mice.

Which, by the way, was *nothing* like how things were in Narnia. At least in the books.

Mom and Dad promised to warn the roofing guys that Mewsie was inside the wall, and not to let them do anything that might end up with him being sealed up inside the wall forever.

But they wouldn't take any of my suggestions as to how to get him out of the wall (such as hiring a professional demolition squad to blast him out. If done delicately, I was sure this would work).

Unlike me, Erica, Caroline, and Sophie were all super excited about our field trip, and especially about our prairie outfits. Caroline loved the nightgown I'd brought her. She put it on right over her T-shirt and leggings, the way I was wearing mine.

And I guess it *was* kind of fun to be wearing nightgowns outside, even though we were fully dressed underneath them. Sophie looked especially silly in hers, since her nightgown had Hello Kitty on it, a pattern that's unlikely a girl in the 1850s would actually have worn, since they didn't have Hello Kitty in those days.

And Erica's mom had insisted on putting Erica's hair in a bun, and sticking a big bow on the top, so she looked a little like a French poodle (though I didn't tell her so, of course. *It's rude to tell someone they look like a French poodle. Unless they are, in fact, a French poodle*).

"You look great, Allie!" my friends kept saying. My mom had done my own hair in braids.

I didn't feel like I looked great, though.

95

I just didn't feel excited about this field trip, like my friends did. I think I was sort of hollow inside. Like the wall Mewsie was hiding in.

"Cheer up, Allie," Caroline said as we walked to school. "I'm sure Mewsie will be fine. And just think about what we've got to look forward to when we get to school!"

What we had to look forward to? Endless boredom? And Mary Kay Shiner?

"A *bus!*" Erica cried, reminding me, knowing my weakness for buses.

"School buses," Sophie said, "are considered the safest vehicles on the road."

This wasn't cheering me up *at all.*

"But there are no seat belts," I reminded her. I said this because I'd been secretly hoping our bus would hit a bump so big, Cheyenne would go flying into the air, her hoopskirt sailing up over her head, and all the boys would see her underwear.

Except that Cheyenne would probably like this.

Although maybe she'd conk heads with Brittany Hauser, knocking them both unconscious.

Then we'd *have* to turn the bus around and come back. And we wouldn't have to sit through any boring bread-baking or kick ball demonstrations!

"But school bus seats are compartmentalized, high-backed, well-padded, and anchored for crash protection," Sophie said, quickly warming to the topic. "And designed with the safety of the occupant in mind, no matter what size. Seat belts could increase the risk of serious neck and abdominal injuries in the case of a crash, and could hamper the bus driver's efforts in helping passengers from making a quick exit from the vehicle."

We all stared at Sophie. She really does read too much about disasters.

Not that I cared. I didn't care about anything. All I wanted was to get this field trip over with as quickly as possible so I could get home to Mewsie.

Oh, Mewsie! If only I had a cell phone! That way I could call Mom a million times during the day to check on Mewsie's progress to make sure he was all right.

"Maybe," Caroline said when I voiced this desire out loud, "it's better that you *don't* have a cell phone, Allie."

When we got to school, we only saw a few people from our class wearing prairie clothes. Elizabeth Pukowski had on a longish dress that you could tell had once been a flower girl dress (that she'd grown out of. She kept pulling at it).

And Joey Fields had rolled his jeans up to his knees to make them look like knickers (of course), and had on a furry hat that he said was made of one hundred percent "real faux coonskin" that his uncle had loaned him.

Elizabeth and Shamira came rushing up to us, laughing — they'd each done their hair in Laura Ingalls braids, like mine — and full of admiration for our look.

"Are those *nightgowns*?" they cried. "That's genius! I wish we'd thought of that!"

So it was kind of hard not to feel proud. Even though the nightgown idea had been Missy's.

But of course we didn't tell anyone that.

And then Rosemary came up to us (not wearing any costume at all, of course), and said, "Allie. Check it out."

She pointed toward the parking lot.

And there it was, all gleaming and yellow. The driver

was leaning against it, drinking a cup of coffee in the sun.

I'll have to admit, my heart skipped a beat.

And it got kind of hard to remember that I had left my cat at home in (maybe) mortal danger, and that in a little while I was going to have to see Mary Kay Shiner and Brittany Hauser and go to what was probably one of the most boring places on earth.

Because I was finally going to be riding on a bus! A real school bus! With windows you could put down and stick your hand out of (even though that was terribly dangerous and probably against the law) and seats you didn't have to buckle yourself into and everything!

When the bell rang, I felt really torn between excitement and dread. Because I knew we wouldn't be marching into school with the rest of the student body.

We'd be marching out to our *bus*.

Which was exciting.

But that bus would be taking us to Honeypot Prairie.

With Mary Kay Shiner.

Horrible.

"All right, class," Mrs. Hunter said, because instead of standing quietly like we were supposed to while waiting in our lines, we were all buzzing with nervous anticipation. "I know how excited you all are to get to Honeypot Prairie . . ."

Uh . . . not really.

". . . and you all look very nice in your period costumes from the eighteen fifties." As she said this, Mrs. Hunter gave a kind smile to me, Caroline, Sophie, and Erica. We all looked at one another and laughed, as did the rest of the class.

"But I still need to take attendance," Mrs. Hunter said. "Which I'm going to do out here, before we lea —"

It was right then that we heard a car door slam.

"Wait!" we heard a familiar voice cry.

We all looked around to see a vision in yellow racing toward us from the car that had just dropped her off.

It was Cheyenne.

But Cheyenne looking as none of us had ever seen her before.

RULE #11

If You Can't Say Something Nice, Just Keep Your Mouth Shut. Really.

Cheyenne had on a hoopskirt, all right, just like she'd said she was going to wear. It was gigantic, sweeping out like a bell all around her, as yellow as a buttercup.

But that wasn't *all* she had on.

No, she also had on a matching yellow jacket (cinched tightly around her waist), a yellow parasol dangling from her wrist, little yellow gloves, and a great big yellow sunbonnet.

Cheyenne looked like something out of a book.

No . . . something out of a *movie.*

We weren't the only ones to see her, though. The whole *school* saw her.

And immediately began whispering about her.

Since this was exactly what Cheyenne had planned by arriving so late (of course), she got exactly what she had always wanted: all the attention from everyone.

"I'm here," Cheyenne yelled, running to her place in line. "Sorry I'm late, Mrs. Hunter. It took forever to get my corset laced up."

"Well," Mrs. Hunter said, staring at her. "I would imagine so."

No one could stop looking at Cheyenne. She wasn't just something from another time:

She was something from another universe.

"Cheyenne," Marianne said worshipfully. She reached out to touch Cheyenne's hair, which she'd curled into ringlets, just like Belle from the movie of *Beauty and the Beast*, in the ball scene. "You look so pretty."

"Oh, thank you," Cheyenne said. She looked out at Patrick Day from beneath her eyelashes. "It was nothing."

But if Cheyenne had expected her new look to make Patrick fall madly in love with her and send *her* flowers, just like that David guy had done to Mrs. Hunter, she was destined to be sadly disappointed.

Patrick turned toward Mrs. Hunter, looking outraged.

"Mrs. Hunter!" he yelled. "Is Cheyenne going to get more extra credit than we are, because her costume is so much fancier?"

Patrick's period costume consisted of a red flannel shirt and jeans, exactly what *we*'d been going to wear before Missy had come up with the nightgown idea!

"No, Patrick," Mrs. Hunter said, checking Cheyenne as present on her attendance sheet. "Everyone gets the same amount of extra credit for effort, no matter how authentic their costume."

Cheyenne sucked in her breath. "But, Mrs. Hunter," she began to whine.

"Ha," Patrick said to her with a sneer. "Good luck fitting onto the bus in *that* thing."

Patrick had a point. It was unclear how Cheyenne was going to fit through the door, let alone into a seat, in her gigantic hoopskirt.

Not that she seemed to care. She was obviously feeling very happy with herself. When she saw us in our nightgowns and aprons, she smirked and asked, "Going to a slumber party?" which sent M and D into gales of hysterical laughter.

Sophie flushed.

"No," she said. "For your information, girls in the eighteen fifties whose fathers were settlers here didn't have very much money, Cheyenne. That's why they *came* here . . . to be farmers, and live off the land. We're just being historically accurate."

"Well, Hello Kitty isn't very historically accurate," Cheyenne said, opening her parasol and twirling it around.

All of our mouths popped open when Cheyenne said that.

Sophie turned even *redder*.

I couldn't believe how mean Cheyenne could be sometimes!

"Come on, you guys," Erica said, rushing in to stop a fight before it started. "It's all just for pretend, anyway."

Cheyenne, and M and D, who weren't even wearing costumes, snickered and turned away.

I could tell it was going to be a long day. That's the thing about girls like Cheyenne and Brittany Hauser and especially my ex-best friend, Mary Kay Shiner: They never learned the rule about how *If you can't say something nice, you should just keep your mouth shut.*

But I didn't have time to think about this (much less write it down in my rules notebook in my backpack) because suddenly:

It was time to get on the bus.

Which we were supposed to do in an orderly manner.

But I can't really say there was anything orderly about the way I latched myself on to Rosemary, or the way we ran for the seat she had told me was one of the best ones: above the rear wheels . . . or the way we catapulted ourselves into it with sighs of relief.

I just couldn't help myself. *Something* good had to come out of this day.

"I was so worried," I said as I sank into the deep padding of the bus seat, "that those guys would get these seats!"

Stuart and Patrick, who had pushed their way ahead of us, Mrs. Hunter having been distracted by Cheyenne not being able (of course) to fit through the bus door with her enormous skirt, had opted for the seats in the last row.

Rosemary looked back at the boys contemptuously.

"Those guys are amateurs," she said. "Those seats are the worst. Especially if someone pukes. No air circulation."

"Wait," I said, freezing. "You think someone is going to throw up?"

"Oh, sure," Rosemary said with a shrug. "On the bus? Someone always does."

No one had ever mentioned someone throwing up on any of the field trips my classes had taken before.

Of course, not having ever been on one myself, I wouldn't have known this.

"Thanks for waiting for us, you guys," Sophie said sarcastically, sinking into the seat in front of us, along with Caroline and Erica. "We got stuck behind Cheyenne."

"Yeah," Caroline said. "It look five minutes to pry her loose."

It seemed to take even longer than that to get everyone

seated (even though our class isn't that big) and for the bus to finally get going. That's because there was some kind of paperwork for Mrs. Hunter to fill out and then give the bus driver, Mr. Curtiss.

As Mrs. Hunter was doing this, I watched her out the window (we were so high up! Bus windows are way higher than the windows of any other sort of car I've ever been in. You can see *everything*).

That's how I noticed something.

"Hey, you guys," I said. "Look at Mrs. Hunter's hand."

Everyone got up on their knees and looked out the bus windows.

"So?" they asked.

"She has a new ring," I said.

It was true. On the third finger of Mrs. Hunter's left hand was a brand-new diamond ring I'd never seen her wear before. It sparkled in the sun as she was signing things on the clipboard Mr. Curtiss had given her.

Elizabeth Pukowski gasped.

"That's an engagement ring," she cried. "Mrs. Hunter is engaged!"

"No, she's not," I said. I have no idea why I said that, though. How would I know whether or not Mrs. Hunter was engaged? Newly engaged people do wear a ring on the third finger of their left hand. Harmony told me this once.

"Yes, she is," Sophie said. "That's an engagement ring. Cheyenne was right! That David guy must have proposed to her. Oh, it's so romantic!"

"You guys," Rosemary said, "are going to make *me* be the one to puke."

I kind of agreed with Rosemary.

"It's a good-quality diamond," Elizabeth Pukowski said. "My uncle is a jeweler, so I would know."

"Stop talking about it," I said. I wished I'd never even brought up the ring. I should have kept it to myself. *The best way to keep people from talking about a certain subject is not to bring it up yourself.* That's a rule.

"Why?" Caroline asked. "It's nice that Mrs. Hunter has found love with an old friend."

No, it wasn't, I thought. *Old things bring nothing but trouble.* That's another rule!

Look at my house:

Because it was old, it had gotten dry rot.

And now the shingles had to be replaced for six thousand dollars, and my cat had disappeared into the wall and wouldn't come out, possibly endangering his life.

And look at this field trip to Honeypot Prairie, an *old* place, where they teach you boring, *old*-timey things that aren't useful to anyone. Because of that, Cheyenne had dressed up like an *old*-timey girl, and was being nasty to everyone.

Not to mention, we were about to go pick up a bunch of my *old* classmates from my *old* school, including my *old* best friend, Mary Kay, who'd ruined my last field trip for me, and was probably going to ruin this one for me, too.

See? Old things only bring trouble!

If you ask me, we should just get rid of everything old!

I especially thought this when the bus — which didn't go over any bumps at *all* the whole way to Walnut Knolls Elementary School, or at least any that I even felt, so I never got to see Cheyenne fly up with her hoopskirt over her head. A total disappointment! — pulled up in front of my old school.

And who should be the first person from my old class to get on it?

None other than Brittany Hauser, who took one look at me and said, "Well, if it isn't Allie Stinkle!"

RULE #12

Old Things Bring Nothing but Trouble

"Allie Stinkle," Patrick Day burst out from the back of the bus. "Good one!"

Brittany glanced at him. I saw her smile.

I could tell this was going to be a *really* terrible day, just as I'd suspected all along.

And who was standing right there behind Brittany? My ex-best friend, Mary Kay Shiner, of course.

She was pretending like she didn't see me.

But I totally knew she did from the smile she had on her face. It was the same smile she'd worn when our third-grade teacher had asked where my permission slip was the morning of our trip to the Children's Museum, and I'd said, feeling my heart explode in terror, "Mary Kay said she handed it in!"

And Mary Kay had said, "Oh, no, Allie. Remember? I gave it back to *you* to hand in."

Only she'd never given it back to me.

I knew exactly what she'd done with it. Lost it. Accidentally (on purpose), of course.

She'd worn the exact same little *I'm sorry (but not really)* smile then that she was wearing now.

Behind Mary Kay were three other girls from my old class — Lauren Freeman, Paige Moseley, and Courtney Wilcox.

Courtney I'd kind of become friendly with ever since Brittany's disastrous birthday party. Courtney had told me she'd only hung out with Brittany and her cronies because there were no other girls in her class with whom to be friends.

Seeing me on the bus now, she smiled at me . . . only not in a fake way like Mary Kay.

I smiled back.

All of the girls, including Brittany and Mary Kay, were wearing period costumes almost as elaborate as Cheyenne's, only they didn't have hoopskirts. They had on white aprons with lace trim that matched the lace on the pantaloons that peeked out beneath the bottom of their gingham prairie dresses. They also had big sunbonnets that hung down their backs from ribbons that matched the color of their dresses.

Brittany's was yellow, like Cheyenne's. Mary Kay's was pink, Lauren's blue, Paige's red, and Courtney's was green.

I could tell they hadn't gotten *those* out of their closets, like we had our costumes. I wondered where they'd found them.

Not to mention how much their parents had paid for them.

Now Brittany looked down at me and said with a smirk, "Nice nightgown, Stinkle."

That was when Cheyenne let out a sharp bark of surprised laughter. Patrick Day and Stuart Maxwell grinned, obviously looking at me in a whole new way . . . like, "This *is the girl who's been telling us to shut up and sit down all year? Allie Stinkle?*"

Why me? I wondered. Really. What had I ever done to deserve all this?

That was when Rosemary, sitting beside me, stood up in her seat. She was nearly six inches taller than most kids our age under normal circumstances.

And standing on the wheel well, she was even taller.

Everyone tilted their chins to look up at her.

"You think things are any different here on the bus than they are in the classroom, shrimps?" she asked Patrick and Stuart. "Allie and I are still in charge!"

Stuart shrank down into his seat. "Sorry," he murmured.

"That's more like it," Rosemary said.

Then she turned to give Brittany — who'd frozen in the middle of the aisle — a look that could have melted a frozen Pine Heights cafeteria Tater Tot.

And those are pretty hard.

"You got a problem with my girl Allie?" Rosemary asked Brittany.

"N-no," Brittany stammered, her eyes huge.

"Good," Rosemary said. "Let's keep it that way. Welcome to my bus."

Brittany blinked a few times. Then she seemed to remember that she's the Cheyenne of her own class.

"It's not *your* bus," Brittany said, sticking out her pointy chin. Which was pretty brave of her, if you thought about it. "Our school paid for half of it."

"Yeah?" Rosemary said. "Well, we got here first. So it's my bus now, unless you want to fight me for it. Which I don't imagine you do, do you, buttercup?"

I heard a few people snicker at Rosemary having called Brittany "buttercup," on account of her yellow dress.

I didn't laugh, though, because I knew what it was like to be threatened by Rosemary. Rosemary had threatened *me* for a while when I'd first started attending Pine Heights. It had been really scary.

Then I'd gotten to know Rosemary, and realized she was actually really lonely, and had wanted me as a friend, and just hadn't known how to ask. . . .

Nevertheless, Rosemary could still be really scary when she wanted to be.

And I didn't think she wanted Brittany as a friend.

Bullying is still wrong, even when it's being done to someone who is a bully herself.

That's a rule.

Still, I was glad Rosemary was my friend.

"What's the holdup back there?" I heard a familiar voice ask from the front of the bus. It was my old teacher, Ms. Myers. Who I used to think was the best teacher in the whole world. Until I met Mrs. Hunter. "Everyone take a seat, please! We need to get on the road for Honeypot Prairie so we'll have plenty of time to enjoy all the activities."

"Here, come sit by us," Cheyenne said, waving. M and D helped shmoosh Cheyenne's hoopskirt down to make room for Brittany. "Don't mind Rosemary. She's all bark and no bite."

"We'll see about that," Rosemary called as Brittany and those guys backed up the aisle to take the seats Cheyenne and her friends were offering. Mary Kay sat down without even looking at me. "Just try that Allie Stinkle bit again and find out."

"Did someone say Allie Stinkle?" called another familiar voice.

I couldn't help letting out a groan.

It couldn't be.

But it was.

I'd recognize that New York accent — not to mention
those freckles and that bright red hair — anywhere.

"Well, well, well." Scott Stamphley dropped into the
seat over the wheel well that was directly across from
the one I shared with Rosemary. "If it isn't my old pal
from the principal's office. Shoved a cupcake into anybody's face lately, Stinkle?"

"Scott," I said. For some reason I could feel my face
turning bright red. I had no idea why. "Shut up."

"I wondered whatever happened to you," Scott went on,
completely ignoring what I'd said about shutting up, as he'd
always used to, back when I'd been forced to be in the same
class with him. "I figured you'd be in prison by now. But
now I see they sent you someplace worse. Pine Heights
Elementary."

117

"You got something against Pine Heights?" Rosemary demanded hotly.

"Simmer down, princess," Scott said. Which was a bit shocking. Mostly because nobody ever calls Rosemary "princess," or "baby girl," or things like that. But also because he didn't seem the least bit scared of her. "I'm not talking to you. I'm talking to Stinkle."

But then Scott got distracted when another boy, Paul Schmitt, raced up, crying, "Dude! You got the seat over the wheels! Awesome!" They started fist-bumping each other.

That's when Sophie's head came popping up over the back of the seat in front of mine.

"Allie," she whispered. "Who is that boy?"

"No one," I said. I had never been so mortified in my life.

Caroline's and Erica's heads joined Sophie's over the back of the seat.

"He's obviously *someone*," Caroline said.

"I think he likes you, Allie," Sophie said. "He wouldn't tease you so much if he didn't like you."

I felt myself turning even redder.

"He doesn't like me," I whispered back. The thought of Scott Stamphley liking me made me feel completely weird inside. "He hates me. He always has. We're total enemies."

"Then why are you blushing?" Sophie wanted to know.

"You know," Rosemary said, looking at me. "You *are.*"

Fortunately at that moment, Mrs. Hunter, at the front of the bus, clapped her hands and asked for our attention. So Sophie and Caroline and Erica had to turn around and stop looking at me.

Thank goodness.

"Children!" Mrs. Hunter said. "We're ready to begin our trip to Honeypot Prairie now! So for those of you from Walnut Knolls Elementary who don't know, let me introduce myself. I'm Mrs. Hunter —"

Then my old teacher, Ms. Myers, stood up and said, "And for those of you from Pine Heights Elementary who don't know *me,* I'm Ms. Myers."

"— and we're so excited you could all join us for what

we're sure is going to be a day of magic, fun, and learning!"
Mrs. Hunter said. "Now, because Honeypot Prairie's interactive exhibitions can better accommodate small groups,
when we get to the park, you'll be splitting up into your
preassigned teams for your tour."

"That means," Ms. Myers said, "Team Miami will tour
the schoolhouse while Team Illini is visiting the blacksmith
shop, while Team Pawnee might be learning how to build
a wigwam, while Team Shawnee might be having an authentic nineteenth-century lunch in the bake house. Then,
within your team, you'll each have a buddy with whom we
want you to stay at all times, for safety. Understand?"

Rosemary held her hand out to me. "Buddies?" she
asked.

"Of course," I said, slipping my fingers into hers.

And not just because I'd seen how awesome she was
around Brittany and those guys.

If I'd learned anything since coming to Pine Heights
Elementary, it was that *You can't have enough buddies.*

And that's a rule.

RULE #13

No Getting up While the Bus Is in Motion

Joey Fields was the one who threw up.

I guess it sort of figured that it would be him.

It was still a surprise. It was as we were going over a really big bump — a pothole on one of the country roads we had to take to get to Honeypot Prairie — that it happened.

Sophie was right: The seats on the school bus really are well padded and compartmentalized for safety. You don't go flying when those back wheels hit something. Not unless you let your body go totally limp, like Rosemary taught me.

That's what I was doing when Joey, who'd been complaining of feeling motion sick, just completely heaved.

The bus driver had to pull over and let us all out so he and Mrs. Hunter could clean it up. Mrs. Hunter kept yelling, "Be careful! Don't step in it!" as we ran off, trying to escape the terrible odor.

But I think a bunch of people stepped in it, anyway, because it still smelled pretty bad when we got back on, even though everyone put their windows down as far as they would go.

Joey felt awful about it. Especially when Brittany and Mary Kay and those guys — who made fast friends with Patrick Day and Stuart Maxwell — started calling him "Chuck." As in "upchuck."

"Hey, nice going, *Chuck*," they kept saying to Joey, when we were back on the bus. "What a magnificent odor you've created, *Chuck*."

Joey already felt bad enough, seeing as how he'd just thrown up. They didn't have to make it worse.

Every time I looked over at him — sitting slumped by himself on a seat (because no one would sit next to the boy who had thrown up . . . not that anyone had wanted to sit next to Joey in the first place, because Joey is also the boy who barks) — I felt really sorry for him. His face was practically green.

Plus, he had his pants rolled up to look like knickers, and that silly hat with the raccoon tail.

It was all just so sad. Almost as sad as me, the girl whose mother doesn't think she's responsible enough to own a cell phone, whose cat won't come out of the wall.

So finally I said, "You guys. Cut it out."

That was when Mary Kay finally said something to me, her ex-best friend, whose chance to see the rare collectible Barbie exhibit she'd ruined.

Mary Kay had just been sitting there in perfect silence the whole time, smiling her stupid, terrible *I'm sorry (but not really)* smile at no one in particular, when all of a sudden, out of nowhere, she piped up with, "What's the matter, Allie? Is Chuck your *boyfriend*?"

Just like that.

Of *course* the minute she said it, Stuart and Patrick were like, "Yeah! Chuck's Allie's boyfriend!"

And Rosemary couldn't get up to pound them into being quiet, because the bus was moving. And Mr. Curtiss had said *No getting up while the bus was in motion*, or he would personally put us off the bus. He didn't care where. It could be the highway. We could just live by the side of the highway, for all Mr. Curtiss cared.

It was Mr. Curtiss's rule.

A part of me couldn't believe Mary Kay had asked such a stupid question. She *knew* Joey wasn't my boyfriend because in the limo to Brittany Hauser's birthday party I'd told her and all those girls that I didn't have a boyfriend.

But another part of me knew exactly why Mary Kay had done it. She'd done it to embarrass me in front of everyone in my (not-so-much-anymore) new school.

Because that's the kind of friend Mary Kay is.

So I was just like, "Yeah, that's right. Joey is my boyfriend," in the most sarcastic voice possible, to show Mary Kay she hadn't embarrassed me at all.

But some people are immune to sarcasm.

Which was why Brittany and Mary Kay and *all* those guys, including Stuart and Patrick and practically half the bus, started singing,

"Stinkle and Upchuck,
sitting in a tree,

K-I-S-S-I-N-G.
First comes love,
then comes marriage,
then comes StinkleChuck
in a baby carriage."

Like this was the most creative, hilarious song in all of
creation.

Which didn't really bother me, because I knew they were
just being stupid. What did I care if they sang a stupid song
about me and Joey kissing and getting married and having a StinkleChuck baby? There's no such thing as a
StinkleChuck baby. And that didn't mean it was going to
come true.

And also, reacting to it would just make them do
it more.

So I ignored it.

And also, I could tell that their singing that song
was making Cheyenne *really* mad, because *all* the boys —
except Scott Stamphley and his friend Paul, who were
trying to play with their Nintendos and looked annoyed

by all the commotion — were paying attention to me and not to *her*.

And anything that made *Cheyenne* mad, made *me* happy. Cheyenne kept looking back from her row on the bus, like, "What is going *on* back there?" and "Why is *Allie* getting all the attention?"

I almost expected Cheyenne to raise her hand and be like, "Mrs. Hunter! Please make the boys pay attention to *me* now."

Only she didn't. Which was almost as disappointing as her hoopskirt not flying up over her head.

The only thing I *was* worried about was Joey.

Because for some reason instead of looking miserable about everyone teasing him about liking me, he looked *happier*.

And I started to suspect that the reason he was happy was because he'd *believed* it when I said he was my boyfriend . . . that I liked him in a lovey-dovey way, not an I-feel-sorry-for-you way.

Which I do *not*.

So then I started worrying that I was going to have *that* to deal with all day, in addition to Mary Kay being such a snot and my worries about Mewsie and Mrs. Hunter and David and the fact that I was wearing a nightgown to school during the daytime.

How do I get myself into these situations? I swear, I was starting to give Uncle Jay's walkabout idea some serious consideration. Maybe I'd just break Mr. Curtiss's rule about getting up from my seat.

Then Mr. Curtiss would put me off on the side of the road, and I could just go looking for my spiritual path.

That would *have* to be preferable to the path I was currently on. Wouldn't it?

Finally, the bus pulled into the parking lot of Honeypot Prairie, and we were able to get off the smelly bus (which Mr. Curtiss promised he was going to take away and properly hose down before we took it back home, so it wouldn't smell of Joey's throw up anymore).

There were four people standing in the parking lot waiting for us. One was dressed like an old-timey blacksmith.

One was dressed like an old-timey schoolteacher. One was dressed liked an old-timey baker.

And the fourth was a lady with really long hair, dressed like an old-timey . . . well, I don't even know *what* she was supposed to be, to tell you the truth.

Each one was holding a sign that said the name of the teams to which we were about to be assigned.

"Oh, *no*," Rosemary said, looking at the old-timey people out the window.

I knew exactly how she felt.

Like going on a walkabout.

"As you get off the bus," Mrs. Hunter yelled, "you'll be handed a slip of paper. That slip of paper will have the name of the team to which you've been assigned. Do not lose that slip of paper!"

"If we're not on the same team," I heard Brittany whisper to Cheyenne, "trade with someone."

"And no trading!" Ms. Myers called out, almost as if she'd overheard. But she couldn't have; there was still so much singing about the StinkleChuck baby. "If we find out you've traded, the punishment will be severe. Remember, we want you to learn to work as a team with people you normally wouldn't get to know!"

"Trade, anyway," I heard Mary Kay say. "I don't want to be on a team with . . . *you know!*"

I knew exactly who she meant, because I saw her gaze dart in the direction of the person she meant.

Me.

I felt my cheeks turning red again.

But this time, it had nothing to do with Scott Stamphley.

I couldn't believe Mary Kay had ever been my friend . . . let alone my *best* friend. What had I ever seen in her? She was a super snob.

Stepping off the bus, I saw the smiling face of my old teacher, Ms. Myers. She was handing out slips of paper to everyone who went by her. When she saw me, her smile broadened.

"Hi, Allie," she said. She remembered me!

"Hi, Ms. Myers," I said, feeling a little shy.

"You look so nice today," she said, meaning my nightgown and apron. "Like a real prairie girl."

"Thanks," I said. See? There was nothing wrong with our period costumes. Brittany and Cheyenne were wrong. We looked nice! Even Ms. Myers thought so.

"Here you go," she said, sticking a slip of paper in my hand.

"Thanks," I said. And looked down at it. *Team Shawnee.*

I glanced around and saw that the schoolteacher lady was holding the sign that said *Shawnee.* Lenny Hsu was standing next to her.

I also saw, to my extreme disappointment, that Scott Stamphley, his friend Paul, Stuart, and Patrick Day were standing next to her.

Great.

Also: Typical that I would get assigned to the team with those guys on it.

Going on a walkabout had never seemed so appealing.

"Hey," I said, turning around to Rosemary. "What did you get?"

"Team Illini," she said. "You?"

"Stupid Team Shawnee," I said.

"I'm Illini, too," Sophie said. Caroline and Erica were both Pawnee.

"No fair," I said. "I'm the only Shawnee?"

"Uh," Rosemary said. "No, you've got plenty of company. Look."

I looked. To my horror, Cheyenne, Brittany, Mary Kay, M and D, *and* Lauren and Paige (but not Courtney) were hurrying toward the schoolteacher lady holding the Team Shawnee sign.

There was no way they *all* could have ended up on the same team.

There was only one answer: They had traded! They had all totally broken the rules, and *traded!* Even though they knew the punishment for breaking the rule was going to be severe!

All the girls were giggling excitedly beneath their bonnet brims and making googly eyes at Scott, Stuart, Patrick, and Paul.

Suddenly, I knew how Joey must have felt on the bus right before he'd heaved. Because I wanted to throw up, too.

"Aw, come on, you guys," I turned around and said to my friends. "No fair. Somebody trade me."

"Oh," Erica said, looking pained. "You know ordinarily I'd do it, Allie. Only, you heard Ms. Myers. No trading."

"Yeah," Caroline said, staring as Cheyenne sashayed up to Scott, opened her parasol, and started twirling it in front of him like she was insane. "Sorry, Allie."

"You can't possibly think any of us would trade with you, Allie," Sophie said, stating the bald truth of the matter, as usual, "after the things you told us about that birthday party you went to with those girls. I mean, there's no way."

Me and my big mouth.

I glanced over my shoulder. Patrick was kicking Cheyenne's hoopskirt to make it sway. Cheyenne shrieked in mock outrage, and darted away. Brittany and Mary Kay laughed hysterically, like this was the funniest thing they'd ever seen in their entire lives.

I couldn't believe *this* was how I was going to have to spend my first-ever field trip. Not only at the world's most boring, *noninteractive* living history museum with *no* Barbies, but with all the people I hated most!

Even though it's wrong to hate people, of course.

"Oh, fine," Rosemary said with a sigh. "I'll do it."

I looked up at her, tears practically shining in my eyes.

"Really, Rosemary?" I cried. "You will?"

"Sure," Rosemary said with a shrug. "I can't stand to see you making that StinkleChuck baby face. What do I care about a bunch of dumb, snobby girls? It's just one day. Besides. We're buddies. Remember?"

I wanted to hug her. Except that Rosemary wasn't exactly the kind of person you hugged.

I thanked her (except . . . what's a StinkleChuck baby face? I wondered) and turned and was about to go running over to Team Illini when I happened to glance back at Team Shawnee one last time.

I really, really wish I hadn't.

Because then I wouldn't have seen what I saw.

RULE #14

It's Important to Make a Big Entrance

What I saw was Joey Fields in his rolled-up pants hurrying over to Team Shawnee, tripping over his own shoelaces (which had come untied, in typical Joey Fields fashion. Why can't he just wear Velcro, like everyone else?) as he was running from the Honeypot Prairie boys' outhouse, where he'd gone to wipe some stray throw up off the tail of his uncle's coonskin hat.

Of course. Of *course* Joey Fields was on the same team as Stuart and Patrick and Cheyenne and Brittany and Mary Kay and all those people who'd been laughing at him all morning during the bus ride.

Because of course *Joey* hadn't broken the rules and traded.

Which meant he was going to get tortured for the rest of the day . . . unless someone was there to stop it.

It was all just so *typical*.

And of course *I'm* the one who'd had to turn around and look just in time to see this.

"Wait," I heard myself say to Rosemary.

She glanced over her shoulder. "What?"

I realized how crazy what I was about to say was going to sound to her. I mean, Joey *wasn't* my boyfriend. I didn't even really like him as a friend. He *barked* instead of talked half the time. What did I care if he got picked on all day?

But I couldn't help remembering the promise I'd made to myself on the way up the steps to Mark's room the night before: that I'd become a more responsible person if Mewsie turned out to be okay.

Well, Mewsie *had* turned out to be okay (even if he was still inside the wall).

And here was my first chance to be a more responsible person.

I couldn't break the rules and trade teams with Rosemary. And I *definitely* couldn't do it if it meant leaving Joey all alone with so many people who were just going to be mean to him.

Because that wasn't what a responsible person — a truly responsible person — would do.

"Never mind," I heard myself saying to Rosemary. It was like my mouth was possessed by someone else! "I guess I don't want to trade after all."

"Okay, whatever," Rosemary said, shaking her head. Then she went to go join Sophie and the other members of Team Illini.

Who were probably going to have the best, funnest day of all time. It was probably going to be like the Dinosphere, SpaceQuest, and Barbie exhibit all rolled into one.

While my own day was going to be like sitting in the principal's office with Mrs. Jones, the administrative assistant, drawing dog pictures.

My own head hanging, I dragged myself over to Team Shawnee.

Really, Stinkle? What are you *doing*? Your first field trip ever, and you're *willingly* sticking yourself on the same team as the boy who threw up on the bus, your two most mortal enemies, your ex-best friend, and *Scott Stamphley*?

This was your chance, Stinkle! Your chance to escape the daily grind, to find your spiritual path, to go on a walkabout!

And you blew it! What's *wrong* with you?

I didn't know. All I knew was, Joey was my responsibility. Mrs. Hunter had stuck me in the back row for a reason: to be a positive influence.

Just because Room 209 was on a field trip didn't mean I could take a walkabout from that.

Which was when I realized, with a sigh, that I was *never* going to go on a walkabout.

Because taking a walkabout when someone needs you is just about the most irresponsible thing you can do.

That was totally a rule.

As I walked over to Team Shawnee — pulling off my apron and my flannel nightgown as I went, because it was getting hot out — the schoolteacher lady was trying to get everyone on Team Shawnee to be quiet by clapping her hands and going, "All right, now, children! Boys and girls! Now, children, we have a lot to learn today. Let's all be quiet so I can tell you about the wonders of Honeypot."

Oh, brother. Did this lady have a lot to learn about kids from modern times. What she really needed was a giant touch-pad screen. Or maybe some animatronic dinosaurs. Or Barbie.

Brittany was saying in her snottiest voice, "So, my parents are *significant* donors to the town community theater. You probably don't know this, but my father owns the local BMW dealership? So anyway, my mother just called the box office and said, 'Listen, if you don't get the costume department to loan my daughter and her friends costumes from last year's production of *Oklahoma!* we're going to pull our support.' And the next thing we knew, an intern brought over these totally adorable costumes —"

Meanwhile, Cheyenne was saying to Brittany, in *just* as snotty a voice, not even listening to her, "Well, I told *my* mother when she called her friend in the retail costume rental business that of *course* I wanted a parasol. With matching fingerless lace mittens! Why *wouldn't* I want that? I mean, only *poor* girls didn't have fingerless lace mittens to match their parasols!"

While this conversation — to which Mary Kay was paying rapt attention — was going on, Scott and his friend Paul were bent over their Nintendos, going, "Yeah! Die! No, you die. No, you! No, you. No, *you!*"

Meanwhile, Stuart and Patrick were kicking up swirls of dirt from the parking lot. The dust clouds were floating over toward Joey Fields, who was bent down, trying to tie his shoes.

"Hey, Chuck," Stuart was saying. Kick. Kick. "How's the weather, Chuck? Any *dust storms* coming, Chuck?"

"Ha-ha," Joey Fields said, coughing from all the dirt. "That's real funny, guys."

"What's that, Chuck?" Patrick said, laughing and kicking dirt. "What did you say, Upchuck?"

"Children," the schoolteacher lady was saying, clapping in a more frantic way. "If you don't behave, we won't have time to play Pom-Pom-Pull-Away!"

That's when I came walking up.

In my reading on how to be a great actress (sometimes I alternate and read about how to be a great veterinarian, since I want to be one of those, too), I've learned that it's important to make a big entrance.

That's why I took my backpack — into which I'd stuffed my wadded-up nightgown and apron, along with my notebook of rules — and threw it down as hard as I could into the dirt next to where Stuart and Patrick were standing.

This made a satisfyingly loud noise. It also caused a large amount of dust to rise up into the air, making Stuart and Patrick cough.

"Oh, no!" I made a very big *Oops!* shrug with my shoulders, like I hadn't meant for this to happen. "Sorry!"

This is called acting.

I wasn't *lying*. There's a difference between lying and acting. Some people don't understand that. Such as Cheyenne.

She came marching over to me, her hands on her corseted waist.

"You did that on purpose, Allie Finkle," she said. "And you know it!"

"No, I didn't," I said, making my eyes all wide and innocent looking. "My backpack just slipped out of my hand."

"Well, I don't believe you," Cheyenne said. "I think you purposefully threw your backpack down to the ground to get Stuart and Patrick all dirty because you're upset about them calling Joey names."

"Probably, considering that he's her boyfriend," Mary Kay said in a loud whisper, with another one of her *I'm sorry (but not really)* smiles.

I really wished that Mary Kay had been standing a little closer to the dirt when I'd slammed my backpack down.

"Really, Allie, that's very immature," Brittany said. "These costumes have to be professionally cleaned, you know."

"Children," the schoolteacher lady said, clapping her hands some more. "Please! If you don't stop this bickering, we won't have time for —"

"Yeah," Patrick said. "You're not the boss of us, Allie *Stinkle*."

"No," said a voice behind us. "She isn't. But I am."

And we all turned to see Mrs. Hunter, her green eyes crackling with anger.

RULE #15

Tattling on People Is Kind of Mean Unless It's for a Good Reason

"Mrs. Hunter," Cheyenne said, pointing at me. "Allie threw her backpack down on the ground on purpose to make a dirt cloud get all over Stuart and Patrick."

Patrick held up his arm. "It's true. Allie got dirt in my scab."

Tattling on people is kind of mean . . .

"Because *they* were kicking dirt on that kid," Scott Stamphley said, pointing at Joey. "And calling him Upchuck."

. . . unless you're tattling on someone for a good reason.

Like Scott tattling on Stuart and Patrick for what they were doing to Joey.

Don't even ask me why Scott Stamphley, of all people, would come to my defense.

Because I honestly have no idea.

Especially since he hates me.

"Really," Mrs. Hunter said, her green eyes crackling even harder. "Well, that hardly sounds like the kind of behavior I would expect from a Team Shawnee member. Perhaps you boys would like to join Mr. Curtiss, spending the rest of the day cleaning the bus floor."

Patrick quickly put his arm down. "I wouldn't like that at all," he said.

"No, thank you," Stuart said, his face starting to turn red.

"Mrs. Hunter," Cheyenne said. "It's true, Stuart and Patrick *were* calling Joey names. But Allie just stomped up and threw her backpack down and got dirt all over them. It was *extremely* rude! You know she has these immature outbursts from out of nowhere *all the time.*"

"I agree," Brittany said. "If I may be frank, I know Allie from when she used to go to Walnut Knolls. And it's always been my observation that she should be held back a year. I mean, she and her friends came to school today in their *pajamas.*"

I felt my face turning as red as Stuart's . . . but for a different reason, of course.

I couldn't believe my trying to do the responsible thing had led to *this.*

Also, I had a very bad feeling that I knew what was coming next:

Mary Kay was going to whisper-shout something about my book of rules.

Why not? I could see her, standing next to Brittany, trying very hard not to look at me. She was staring at the ground, the rim of her bonnet hiding her face.

But it was obvious that she was just aching for the right moment to spill the beans again about my very private and personal business. She'd already told everybody Joey was my boyfriend (a total lie).

What was keeping her from telling everyone something that was actually true?

Well, if she opened her mouth about it, I decided, I was going to tell on all of *them* for trading teams, even though Ms. Myers had forbidden it. Those girls had to have traded to all end up on Team Shawnee like this. Mrs. Hunter *had* to be able to see this. Maybe she didn't know that Brittany and Mary Kay and Lauren and Paige were all friends.

But she *obviously* knew that Cheyenne and Marianne and Dominique were. She *had* to do something about it. It wasn't fair —

Except that before I got a chance to say anything about it, Mrs. Hunter said, "Well, if *I* may be frank, ladies, I'd like to make an observation of my own. And that's that I'm not seeing very much teamwork at all here on Team Shawnee. In fact, I'm seeing the opposite of that. So I think I'll take it upon myself to see if I can't do a little something about that."

"Oh," Cheyenne said quickly. "We're practicing team-work, Mrs. Hunter. See?"

And she put her arm around Brittany's waist and cocked her head in a way that looked a lot like Kevin's cute face.

"How nice," Mrs. Hunter said. "But that isn't exactly the kind of teamwork I had in mind. It's my understanding that part of the Honeypot Prairie experience is getting to know your neighbors, just like the early settlers did, back when they needed one another's help with putting out wildfires and fending off attacks from wild boars. Isn't that so, Mrs., er . . ."

"Higginbottom," the schoolteacher lady said. "And it certainly is." She nodded so hard, her bun fell down.

I saw Cheyenne exchange glances with M and D. Brittany did the same with Mary Kay, Lauren, and Paige.

I could pretty much read their thoughts. They were thinking the same I was:

Wild boars? What was about to happen here?

"So I think the best thing to do," Mrs. Hunter said, "would be to assign each of you a buddy right now, someone for you to spend the rest of the day with, someone for you to get to know *much* better —"

"Exactly," Mrs. Higginbottom said enthusiastically. "I think this is a splendid idea."

"Great," Mrs. Hunter said.

This was when my heart gave a great big unhappy *plop.* Because I could tell what Mrs. Hunter was about to do.

And I wasn't going to like it. *No one* was.

Not at all.

"You," Mrs. Hunter said, pointing at Brittany. "You're going to be his buddy."

Then she pointed at Lenny Hsu.

"What?" Brittany's face, beneath her bonnet brim, fell.

Lenny, glancing up from the book on dragons he'd been deeply engrossed in during all of this, didn't seem too happy about the arrangement, either.

"You," Mrs. Hunter said, pointing at Patrick. "You're going to be *her* buddy."

And she pointed at Paige.

Paige looked like she was going to be the second person on the field trip to throw up.

"Do I have to?" she asked anxiously.

"Well," Mrs. Hunter said. "You traded to be on this team. Didn't you?"

Paige looked a little faint.

"We told you the punishment for trading was going to be severe," Mrs. Hunter said.

Oh, this was severe, all right. It was even worse than wild boars.

"Excuse me," Cheyenne said, raising her hand, even though we weren't in class. "I volunteer to be *his* buddy."

And she pointed at Scott Stamphley, her other hand going to her ringlets as she smiled at him adoringly.

Scott Stamphley turned as red as my nightgown.

Then he stepped quickly toward Joey, the person standing closest to him (besides his friend Paul). "I volunteer to be *his* buddy," he said, indicating Joey.

Mrs. Hunter hesitated. It was pretty clear she was punishing everyone by not letting anyone be buddies with someone they actually *wanted* to be buddies with. So Scott volunteering to be buddies with Joey was screwing up her whole plan.

Joey looked up at Scott — who was almost a head taller than he was — and said, in a worshipful voice, "I'll be your buddy, Scott."

"Fine," Mrs. Hunter said. "If that's what you want, Joey. You two be buddies."

I was pretty sure Mrs. Hunter was letting Joey pick his own buddy because he'd been the one who'd thrown up on the bus that morning.

Still, Scott Stamphley couldn't be Joey's buddy! Scott Stamphley was . . . Scott Stamphley. He wasn't going to be a positive influence on Joey. Scott Stamphley was going to show Joey how to fart and then wave the fart smell in my direction. Scott Stamphley was going to teach Joey how to burp the alphabet. Scott Stamphley was going to show Joey how to flip his eyelids inside out and then tap unsuspecting girls on the shoulder and say, "Hello, may I borrow your pencil?"

These were all things I had seen Scott Stamphley do in the past.

He just hadn't done any of them *today*.

And so Cheyenne, who didn't know any better, had a crush on him.

And Mrs. Hunter, who hadn't seen him do any of these things, thought he might be a positive influence like me!

But before I could warn her, Mrs. Hunter was pairing off everyone else in our group, so quickly that I hardly had time to register it when I heard, "All right, boys and girls!"

Mrs. Higginbottom made her voice all mysterious. "Follow me back into eighteen forty-nine . . . when there was no electricity. . . . There were no cars . . . no ice for your drinks, because there was no such thing as refrigeration . . . and let's go . . . to the Honeypot schoolhouse!"

And Mrs. Hunter had us get into line two-by-two so we were standing next to our buddy . . .

And I found myself right next to my ex-best friend, *Mary Kay Shiner!*

RULE #16

Speak Not Injurious Words, Neither in Jest nor Earnest

"I don't like this any more than you do, Allie," Mary Kay whispered as we sat in the desk we were being forced to share (in olden times, there weren't enough desks for every student to have her own, so everyone had to share). "But we have to do it, or we'll get into trouble. So let's just make the best of it."

Make the best of it? I had to share a desk with the whiniest girl in the world . . . a girl who'd stabbed me in the back and betrayed me . . . and then gone over to the side of the enemy? *Multiple times?*

And she wanted me to *make the best of it?*

"Oh, right," I whispered back. "You know, I forgave you about the thing with the Children's Museum —"

"Can't you let that go?" Mary Kay whispered. "I told you, I lost your permission slip." Except that she'd lost it *on purpose*. And never told me until it was too late. "Why would you give something that important to someone else, anyway?"

"Fine," I said. What was the point? "But that Barbie exhibit left town and I never did get to see it."

"Are you *still* going on about that?" Mary Kay rolled her eyes. "God, I can't believe you even care. It's just Barbie! Brittany's right. You're so immature."

I felt tears prick my eyes. It wasn't just that it was Barbie. That wasn't even the point.

"What about you telling everyone about my book of rules?" I demanded beneath my breath.

"Well." At least Mary Kay had the decency to blush beneath the rim of her bonnet. "Who even *does* something like that? Keeping a book like that is just weird."

"It's not weird," I whispered back. "Lots of people keep journals."

"Sure," Mary Kay whispered. "Journals. Not *books of rules*. Only a freak would do that, Allie."

"Ladies?" Mrs. Higginbottom clapped her hands at us from the front of the room. "Is there a problem?"

"No, ma'am," we both said at the same time, straightening up in our desk. I guess we *had* been talking kind of intensely during her long speech about the history of the Honeypot Prairie schoolhouse, which hadn't had heat *or* electricity until the 1950s. If the teacher or students had wanted light or warmth, they'd had to gather around the potbellied stove in the middle of the room.

Like I cared.

"Well, then," Mrs. Higginbottom said. "Since you're feeling so chatty, I'm sure one of you won't mind taking a trip to the recitation bench and reading aloud from this McGuffey Reader. . . ."

She held out a beat-up old book.

Great. We were busted.

Because Mary Kay's face turned a deep shade of umber (which is darker than red) and her eyes instantly filled with tears, I knew it was up to me to save the day.

Again.

Really, what would Mary Kay do without me?

And as usual, she wasn't the least little bit grateful.

I took the book and stood up, going to the bench Mrs. Higginbottom had pointed out. I will admit, my heart gave a big thump as I climbed up onto it. It was high . . . and a lot like climbing onto a stage.

Then again, I love being onstage! And because this isn't *really* the 1850s, I can totally be a veterinarian slash actress when I grow up, like I want to.

So I don't really know why I was so nervous all of a sudden.

Maybe it was because of the venue — which is theater talk for the place where I was performing. The inside of the schoolhouse at Honeypot Prairie was even worse than the kids in Mrs. Danielson's class had described it. I mean, it was *old*. It *looked* old. It *smelled* old. There was nothing interactive about it.

It was just one big room (which is I guess why they called it a one-room schoolhouse), filled with desks, built around that potbellied stove. All the kids who lived on Honeypot Prairie, no matter what age, had had to go to class in the *same* room, from the kindergartners to the high school kids.

The teacher had had to run around, teaching all the classes one at a time, giving each grade a different assignment to work on before turning to teach the next group.

If you ask me, it's amazing anyone learned anything at all. I mean, what if there'd been a Patrick Day or Scott Stamphley in the schoolroom? Or my brother Kevin, for goodness' sake, demanding that everyone admire his hard hat? How much work do you think anyone would have gotten done with *Kevin* around, putting on his cute face?

Mrs. Higginbottom had explained to us as we came in, however, that in the 1850s, it hadn't been unusual for teachers to employ corporal punishment . . .

. . . which meant switches, a type of spanking done with a stick or ruler, to keep unruly children in order.

When she'd said *that*, I'd turned in my seat to give Stuart and Patrick and those other boys a *look*.

But Scott Stamphley, at least, was being . . . well, good. There was no other way to describe it.

He was sitting in the desk he and Joey Fields were sharing, with his gaze glued to Mrs. Higginbottom, not fidgeting or looking out the windows or trying to distract any of the other kids by making peeping noises (like he used to do back in Ms. Myers's classroom).

If I hadn't known him better, I'd have thought he was a perfect angel . . . a real Lenny Hsu type.

Maybe he'd turned into a positive influence (like me) since I'd moved to Pine Heights.

On the other hand . . . how likely was that? Knowing Scott, not very.

More likely, he was just waiting until Mrs. Hunter finally went away to go check on some other team before he made his move. . . .

Patrick was being similarly well behaved . . . well, sort of. He was trying to sit as far away from Paige — who was sitting as far away from *him* as *she* possibly could — on the bench they were sharing. Really, it was like Paige didn't want any part of her body or clothes to accidentally brush up against Patrick . . .

. . . while Brittany was pulling the same stunt with Lenny Hsu.

It was like both girls were convinced the boys had head lice.

Cheyenne, meanwhile, looked the most miserable of anybody in the room.

This was because her buddy, at least for the time being, was Mrs. Hunter.

Under normal circumstances I'm pretty sure Cheyenne would have *loved* having so much attention from a teacher all to herself.

But today for some reason it really seemed to be bothering her. She kept looking over at where Scott was sitting, and laughing really loud in this fake way at things Mrs. Higginbottom had said, then tossing her ringlets like she was trying to get him to look in her direction.

But he totally wouldn't turn his head. Scott didn't seem very interested in Cheyenne.

"Go on, dear," Mrs. Higginbottom said to me when I'd straightened up on the recitation bench. "Starting with Lesson One. This is a *real* recitation that a student your age might have had to perform back in eighteen forty-nine," Mrs. Higginbottom assured everyone in the schoolroom.

I could tell from everyone's glazed expressions that no one could have cared less. I knew *I* certainly couldn't. I bet everyone was wishing as hard as I was that we were in the nice, air-conditioned SpaceQuest planetarium (with a DigiStar sky projection system in 3-D) at the Children's Museum instead of stuck inside this stupid one-room schoolhouse on this hot spring day with the sun blazing down outside the windows.

"Okay," I said, holding up the frayed, yellowed book. "Here goes. 'George Washington's Rules of Civility and Decent Behavior in Company and Conversation. Rule the First: *Every Action done in Company, ought to be with Some Sign of Respect, to those that are Present.*'"

"Do you understand what that means, children?" Mrs. Hunter asked from the back of the room. "It means that when you're in the company of others, you ought to be respectful and courteous of them. Go on, Allie."

"'Rule the Second,'" I read. "*'When in Company, put not your Hands to any Part of the Body, not usually Discovered. . . .'*"

"That means," Mrs. Hunter said, casting a look at Patrick, "when you're with other people, do not stick your hands down your pants or your finger up your nose."

Everyone from Room 209 laughed. This was because Patrick was always sticking his finger up his nose, and wiping whatever he found in there on whatever was handy (or even eating it sometimes, if no one was looking).

It wasn't because of this that I lowered the book, though.

Smiling, Mrs. Higginbottom made a "go on, you're doing fine" motion with her hand.

I lifted the book and read some more.

"'Rule the Third,'" I read. "'*Show Nothing to your Friend that may affright him.*'"

"That means —" Mrs. Hunter began to translate.

"Oh, I know," Cheyenne said, raising her hand. "Don't scare your friends!"

"Correct," Mrs. Hunter said. "Go on, Allie."

"Wait," I said.

I was in total and complete shock. I just needed some clarification.

"George Washington — our country's first president," I said, "*wrote a book of rules?*"

My voice cracked. That's how astonished I was.

"Oh, my, yes," Mrs. Higginbottom said with a surprisingly girlish giggle for someone as old as she was. "And when he was a very young man. They might seem a little old-fashioned to you children today, but they're actually just common-sense advice about showing respect for others and in turn, respecting oneself. George Washington's *One Hundred and Ten Rules of Civility & Decent Behavior* was required reading for all pupils at Honeypot Prairie Schoolhouse. If they didn't memorize them by second grade, they didn't pass to third grade."

I couldn't believe it.

So I *wasn't* a freak, as my ex-best friend, Mary Kay Shiner, had suggested just minutes earlier!

The very first president of our country had *also* kept a book of rules when he was a kid . . . a book so famous that schoolchildren had once been forced to memorize it!

From my perch on top of the recitation bench, I looked down at Mary Kay, Brittany, and all the other girls who had been so mean to me that day at Walnut Knolls Elementary, when the truth had gotten out about my own book of rules.

What did they think about *that*, I wondered? That our very first president had kept a book of rules when he'd been a kid . . . *just like me?*

Especially, I wondered, Rule the Forty-ninth, which I'd already skipped ahead and looked at:

Use no Reproachful Language against any one, neither Curse nor Revile?

I guess *I* wasn't the weird one, after all! Not if a famous president had done the exact same thing I was doing!

"Can I keep this?" I asked Mrs. Higginbottom excitedly, holding up the reader.

"Oh, no, dear," she said, trying to take the book out of my hands, her expression a little suspicious, like she was afraid I might try to steal it. "That's Honeypot Prairie property. You can find a copy of George Washington's rules online, you know, for free. It's not copyrighted material."

I had no idea what she was talking about. All I knew was, I wanted to keep reading the president's rules all day, and see how they matched up to mine.

It was like President George Washington and I were *practically the same person.*

"It's all right, dear," Mrs. Higginbottom said, tugging on the book. "You can let go of the reader now. Your turn on the recitation bench is over."

I realized I was still holding the book.

"Can't I," I said, tightening my grip, "just borrow it for the rest of the time I'm here? I'll give it back before we leave Honeypot Prairie. I promise."

"No," Mrs. Higginbottom said, tightening her grip as well. She also dropped her fake old-timey accent. "We need it for the next team of children who come in here."

"Mrs. Higginbottom," Mrs. Hunter said, getting up from the desk she was sharing with Cheyenne. "Hadn't we better hurry up if we're going to make it to the bake house in time for lunch?"

Mrs. Higginbottom looked at the gold watch pinned to the decorative waistband of her long skirt and cried, "Oh, dear, yes. But we didn't have time to make our kick ball of rock and string! Or play Pom-Pom-Pull-Away. Darn it!"

I was pretty sure everyone on Team Shawnee was going to be able to overcome their disappointment.

Especially when the man in the old-timey baker's costume appeared in the schoolhouse doorway, blocking out all the light behind him, because he was so big, and demanded, his arms covered in flour, "Team Shawnee! Are you ready to *eat*?"

I hadn't realized until that moment how hungry I was. Time was kind of flying by, now that things at Honeypot Prairie had actually started getting interesting.

"Yeah," most of us shouted back to him in response to his question.

"Well, then get to the bake house," he roared. "Because nobody who lived on Honeypot Prairie in eighteen forty-nine ate unless they made their bread themselves!"

RULE #17

Use No Reproachful Language Against Any One

Even someone who'd been expecting to have as bad a time at Honeypot Prairie as I had would have to admit that Master Baker Sean put on a pretty good presentation.

Okay, it wasn't in 3-D.

And he didn't have a giant touch-pad screen.

And there weren't any animatronic dinosaurs.

He just showed us how the early settlers had smushed the wheat they'd grown (using a grinding mill) to make it into flour, then added water and yeast to make it into dough.

I already knew about the dough part because of Uncle Jay letting my brothers and me make our own dough at Pizza Express, where he works (and also Caroline's dad's girlfriend, Wei-Lin, letting us make dim sum that one time).

But I didn't know about milling wheat. Cheyenne and Brittany took especially long turns at the grinding mill, saying things like, "It's so hard!" and "I can't do it!" even though it was totally easy to work the crank. When they got done, they kept giggling and saying "how cute" they thought Master Baker Sean was in his apron.

I swear they both made me feel as sick as if I were Lauren Freeman, who'd announced she was wheat gluten–intolerant (Master Baker Sean had some special non-wheat flour for her).

While we waited for the little loaves of bread we'd made to bake, Master Baker Sean took us out behind the bake house. There, Honeypot Prairie was growing the kind of fruit trees and vegetables early settlers would actually have depended on for food back in the 1800s.

Okay, it wasn't a path through a jungle simulated to be exactly like it was during the Cretaceous period more than sixty-five million years ago.

But it was kind of cool to walk around the garden and orchards while Master Baker Sean told us what the different plants and flowers were.

My mom is trying to grow a garden at our house, with things like carrots and lettuce and tomatoes (yuck) in it. Except that squirrels (and Marvin) keep getting into it.

People didn't get bored of Master Baker Sean, because he said things like, "Locust infestations were a major bummer back then, dude" and "Nobody can stand a barley midge, man."

And everyone seemed to have fun after the garden and orchard tour, putting together our own sandwiches from the bread we'd made ourselves with stuff grown or preserved on Honeypot Prairie.

It was as we were sitting at picnic tables on Honeypot Prairie Common, finishing up lunch, getting ready to go over to the stables to see how the blacksmith shod a horse, that everything fell apart.

Maybe it was because there was so much sugar in the homemade lemonade the Honeypot Prairie people gave us to drink with our traditional prairie lunch of sandwiches, kettle chips, and apples.

Maybe it was because some of us still hadn't worked off all our pent-up energy from when we'd been sitting in the schoolhouse, listening to Mrs. Higginbottom.

Or maybe it was because we hadn't gotten to play Pom-Pom-Pull-Away.

But if you ask me, it was because Mrs. Hunter got a call on her cell phone and said, "Oh, excuse me, I have to take this, I'll just be a minute," and walked way to the bottom of the orchard, her face glowing in a special way that I could tell meant that call wasn't business. It was personal.

But all of a sudden, it seemed like everyone on Team Shawnee went nuts.

"Hey, Upchuck," Stuart said, suddenly snatching the coonskin hat off Joey Fields's head. "Nice hat. I think I'll keep it."

Then Stuart put Joey's hat on his own head.

Patrick Day started smirking like this was the funniest thing he'd ever seen or heard. Cheyenne and Brittany and

all of the other girls, with the exception of myself, followed suit.

"Hey, now," Master Baker Sean said, not certain what
was going on . . . but knowing something other than a
locust infestation was happening, and looked up from the
bees he was swatting away. I'll say one thing about Honeypot
Prairie: It lived up to its name. There were a *lot* of bees . . .
especially around the cups of lemonade we were drinking.
They seemed to really want to dive on in there and take a
couple of swigs themselves. "Everybody simmer down, now.
Blacksmith Todd is going to be here in a minute, and you
guys aren't going to want to miss that —"

"Oh, what's the matter?" Stuart asked, ducking as Joey
reached for his hat. "Want it back?"

"Yes," Joey said. I could hear the beginning of a bark in
his voice. "It's not mine. It's my uncle's. It's his favorite hat.
He only let me borrow it as a special favor on the condition
that I not lose it."

"Well," Stuart said. "That's too bad. Because it's
mine now."

Joey looked like he was about to cry.

"Really, Joey," Cheyenne said. "Don't be so immature."

I was sitting at the same picnic table as Cheyenne, with Brittany and her "buddy" Lenny and my "buddy" Mary Kay.

Not that I *wanted* to sit with Mary Kay. But I hadn't had much of a choice, with Mrs. Hunter watching.

Except that Mrs. Hunter was gone, still off on her cell phone, talking to her new fiancé.

That's when I put my cup of too-sugary lemonade — Honeypot Prairie definitely didn't use a mix — down with a thump that made it slosh and a lot more bees rush over to have a few licks.

"Cheyenne," I said. "Shut up." To Stuart I said, "Give him his hat back."

Stuart widened his eyes at me. "Ooooh," he said, pretending, in the words of President Washington, to be affrighted. "What are you gonna do about it?"

Brittany decided to join in, too.

"Look out, Stuart," she said. "Stinkle doesn't want anyone messing with her boyfriend!"

"Stinkle and Upchuck, sitting in a tree," Stuart began to sing again, just like on the bus, taking the hat off and tossing it to Cheyenne.

"K-I-S-S-I-N-G," everyone — with the exception of Lenny and Joey and me and Master Baker Sean, who still just looked confused — joined in, tossing the hat back and forth.

"First comes love —"

Around and around went Joey's uncle's hat, as he darted back and forth, fighting back tears, trying to get it back, but never quite being able to reach it.

"Then comes marriage —"

I tried to help Joey get his uncle's hat back, and so did Lenny. But of course, people caught on that that was what we were doing, and didn't toss it in our direction.

"Then comes StinkleChuck in the baby —"

A hand reached up and snatched Joey's uncle's hat, right out of Marianne's grasp, taking her by surprise.

"Here," Scott Stamphley said, giving Joey his uncle's hat back. He'd just emerged from the bake house water closet, where I totally hadn't noticed he'd been all this time.

Joey took the hat and shoved it back onto his head.

"That wasn't funny, you guys," he said. "Grrr. Ruff!"

Scott gave Stuart a super mean look. I don't know how he knew Stuart had been the one to start it, since he hadn't even been around when Stuart had done it.

"Were you messing with my buddy?" Scott asked Stuart.

Scott looked mad enough that, if I had been Stuart, I'd have lied.

But Stuart just laughed and said, "Oh, come on. We were just having some fun."

Brittany laughed in a super shrill way. "Totally. I mean, what do you expect, Scott? He goes to *Pine Heights!*"

"What's wrong with people who go to Pine Heights?" Cheyenne wanted to know.

"Well, no offense," Brittany said. She was still laughing a little. "But everyone knows Pine Heights is the worst school in the whole *town*. I mean, nobody with any *brains* would go there. If they could help it, anyway."

She and everyone else who went to Walnut Knolls laughed. Except Scott.

I guess Scott must also follow President Washington's Rule the Forty-ninth about not speaking injurious words — or using reproachful language — against others.

"Um," Cheyenne said, exchanging glances with M and D. "Excuse me. But *we* go there. Are you suggesting *we* don't have any brains?"

"Well," Brittany said sympathetically, "you guys can't help it that your families all live on the poor side of town."

"Ex*cuse* me?" Cheyenne said.

I think it's probably safe to say that this was the first time I ever actually agreed with Cheyenne about something. And that was that Brittany had better shut her mouth. And fast.

Except that she didn't, of course.

"Well," Brittany said. But she didn't look as sure of herself as before. "Pine Heights doesn't exactly have the kind of resources and facilities *my* parents would want for me, or expect from an educational —"

"Oh, my gosh," Cheyenne interrupted. Her jaw

had dropped. "I think you just said you're better than I am."

Brittany blinked a few times. "No. That's not what I —"

"They think they're better than we are," Cheyenne said to M and D.

"They totally do," M said.

"No girl in a *bonnet*," D said, folding her arms across her chest, "is going to tell me I'm poor."

I didn't say anything out loud.

But again, I was amazed to find myself in complete agreement with Cheyenne, and even with her friends, Marianne and Dominique.

"I didn't mean *you're* poor," Brittany said. She looked over at Mary Kay and Lauren and Paige for help. "I just meant your *school* is. Right, guys? I mean, *everyone* knows —"

Scott Stamphley was shaking his head at Brittany.

"You've really," he said in disgust, "done it now, Brit."

"Hey, now," Master Baker Sean said, sounding nervous. "I think I hear Blacksmith Todd coming!"

"I mean, it's *kind* of true," Lauren said. "What Brittany said. Isn't it true your cafeteria is also the gym?"

"Um, yeah," Paige said. "And isn't your gym *also* the auditorium? Where the stage is?"

This was all totally true. Walnut Knolls Elementary not only has a separate cafeteria, auditorium, and gym, it has a *boys'* gym, and a *girls'* gym, for when the kids there are doing gymnastics versus basketball.

Pine Heights only has one giant room for all of that. So often, when we are having gym, we end up doing cartwheels on top of squashed Tater Tots.

Now that I thought about it, Pine Heights was kind of the one-room schoolhouse of our town.

"But that," I heard myself saying loudly, "doesn't make Pine Heights a bad school."

"I didn't say it was a bad school, Allie," Brittany said all snottily. "Don't put words in my mouth."

"Uh," Scott Stamphley said. "Actually, Brittany, your exact words were that it's the worst school in the whole town."

"And that's not even true," Cheyenne said, thrusting out

her chin. "Because how many kids from *your* school went on to the regionals in the district spelling bee, if it's so great? Because Lenny here almost did, and our other classmate, Caroline Wu, actually did."

Cheyenne had a point. I couldn't believe I'd forgotten about that. Pine Heights may not be the fanciest school in our town. But the kids who go there, my friends, are certainly the smartest.

"Um," Brittany said, her mouth opening and closing rapidly. "Well . . ."

"Hello there, young'uns," called a large man in a leather apron as he strode up to us. Team Illini was trailing along behind him, looking excited, probably because they knew they were about to get to lunch. I saw Rosemary and Sophie. They smiled at me and waved, not having any idea they were about to walk into a giant fight. "Who all is ready to see some horses?"

"What," Rosemary asked, coming to stand next to where I was sitting at my picnic table, "is going on over here? Why does everyone look so mad?"

"Oh," I said. "No reason. Those Walnut Knolls kids just

think our school is old and falling down and that we're all stupid and poor. That's all."

Rosemary sucked in her breath and glanced at Brittany.

"*What* did you say about our school?" she demanded.

It was amazing what a mere *look* from Rosemary could do.

"It was all just a misunderstanding," Brittany stammered. "I didn't know what I was talking about!"

"I'll tell you something about Walnut Knolls," Rosemary roared. "It's —"

It was at that exact moment that Mary Kay, sitting next to me, jumped up and let out a scream loud enough to wake the ghost of every settler who had ever lived at Honeypot Prairie.

RULE #18

Show Nothing to Your Friend That May Affright Him

"You guys!" cried Mary Kay. She turned wide and frightened eyes toward Brittany and her friends. "Something . . . something . . . *OW!*"

Mary Kay wasn't exaggerating, for once. Something had very definitely done *something* to her. Her face was as pink as the gingham on her dress, and tears were streaming down her face.

That wasn't particularly unusual for Mary Kay, since she cries all the time . . . or at least she used to, back when I'd been best friends with her.

But she was also hopping up and down. And waving her hands in front of her face. And going, "Ow, ow, ow, ow, ow."

That wasn't the kind of thing she used to do, back in the old days.

Not unless she was really hurt.

And the fight that I knew was coming between our two schools — Pine Heights and Walnut Knolls — hadn't even started yet. No one had laid a finger on her.

So what was the matter with her?

Maybe she was just getting the crying and screaming over with in advance?

This was exactly the sort of thing Mary Kay *would* do. Although she and her friends like to call me immature, the truth is, *they* are the ones who are kind of big babies.

Then I looked down to where Mary Kay had been sitting next to me a few seconds before.

And I knew exactly what was going on.

"Oh, my gosh," I said, leaping up from my seat. "Mary Kay, let me see your face."

But Mary Kay wouldn't hold still, because she was still jumping up and down and waving her hands so much. Finally, I grabbed her by both shoulders and *forced* her to stand still so I could get a good look at her.

And there it was.

"Mary Kay," I said, trying to appear calm. Because that's the rule about what you're supposed to do in the face of a medical emergency. "You're going to be all right. But . . . a bee stung your face."

"*What?*"

Mary Kay wasn't the only one who screamed when I said that. Brittany — and everyone else who saw the same thing I did at the same *time* I did — screamed, too.

Screamed and ran away.

Because they could all see the stinger the bee had left behind, sticking out of the middle of Mary Kay's chin.

Mary Kay started to reach up to her face.

"No," Sophie cried. She was the only one besides me and the boys (including Master Baker Sean and Blacksmith Todd) who hadn't run away. "Don't touch it! You'll just make it worse. We need to get it out right away, before the venom has a chance to spread."

Sometimes, I thought, Sophie could be a little *too* graphic.

Because this just made Mary Kay shriek even louder. So loud I thought my eardrums would split in two.

"It's still in there?" Mary Kay wailed, flailing her hands around. "You guys!" She flung a desperate look over at Brittany and Lauren and Paige. "*Help me!* Get it out, get it out, get it *out*. . . ."

But Mary Kay's friends from Walnut Knolls wanted nothing to do with her and her gross bee sting with the venom sac still attached. They looked totally freaked out and scared. *I* was the one who had to swat Mary Kay's hands away to keep her from knocking the stinger in even deeper.

And Mary Kay and I hadn't even been speaking for, like, a year, practically.

"Also," Sophie said, turning to Master Baker Sean and Blacksmith Todd. "You need to get everyone else out of here. When a bee stings someone, it releases a scent to let the rest of the hive know there's danger, and then they'll come to sting anyone else they think might be a threat —"

This caused even more screaming. People were running around like ants from an anthill someone had stomped on.

Especially, I'm sorry to have to say, Mary Kay's friends. Seeing this, Mary Kay wailed even louder.

"Okay, Team Illini," Master Baker Sean started yelling and waving his arms. "Inside the bake house! Now!"

"Team Shawnee!" Blacksmith Todd cupped his hands over his mouth and called. "Follow me to the stables!"

Because Honeypot Prairie is called Honeypot Prairie for a reason.

There are a lot of beehives on it.

This, I thought to myself, is a *disaster*.

Then, as if she'd heard my thoughts, Mrs. Hunter appeared at my side.

"Don't worry," she said soothingly to Mary Kay. "Everything is going to be fine."

Mrs. Hunter had taken a credit card from her wallet. Now she scraped it across Mary Kay's chin — before Mary Kay even knew what was happening and could scream for her to stop — removing the stinger and venom sac in one fell swoop.

"There," Mrs. Hunter said. "All better."

Mary Kay was super surprised for a second . . . then she just cried harder. I think it was a combination of the pain and the shock and knowing all her friends had deserted her in her time of need.

"Ow," she cried, feeling the bump on her chin where the stinger had been. It was already red and getting swollen. "It really hurts."

"Oh, sweetheart," Mrs. Hunter said, giving her a hug. "I know. But it's going to be better now, uh . . ."

". . . Mary Kay," I said, because it was clear Mrs. Hunter was waiting for Mary Kay to tell her her name.

And it was also clear Mary Kay was never going to do so, because she was crying too hard from pain and being scared.

"Right," Mrs. Hunter said. "Mary Kay, have you ever been stung by a bee before? Are you allergic?"

"She's not allergic," I said. Mary Kay was still crying

too much to answer any questions. "I mean, she stepped on a bee at the pool last summer, and she wasn't allergic then."

This just made Mary Kay cry even louder, remembering how "mean" the lifeguard had been (in her opinion) for not carrying her to the infirmary afterward. She'd made her limp on her own.

"Well," Mrs. Hunter said. "That's good. But I think we should call your parents, anyway. They might think it's a good idea for you to see a doctor —"

"There's a first aid kit in the administrative office," said Blacksmith Todd, not talking in an old-timey way anymore. He'd shepherded most of Team Shawnee far enough away from the picnic tables that a bee attack didn't look like it would be a problem. "With EpiPens in children's doses."

"Do you think someone could run and find Ms. Myers," Mrs. Hunter said, "while I take Mary Kay to the office? I think she's with Mistress Carol at the wigwams."

"I'll do it," Scott Stamphley said, raising his hand. What was he still doing here? He was the only other kid who had stuck around (besides me and Sophie) when Sophie had said what she had about the hive attacking. How come he was always popping up when I least expected it?

"Thank you," Mrs. Hunter said to Scott. To Mary Kay, she said, "Come on, honey. Why don't we go to the office and call your parents and put some ice on that bite? It looks like it's swelling."

"I don't want t-to g-go alone," Mary Kay sobbed. "C-can't one of my friends come with me?"

I looked at Mrs. Hunter, who looked back down at me. I could read what Mrs. Hunter's look said, even though she hadn't said anything out loud. The look said, *Uh-oh.*

Because all of Mary Kay's friends had left the picnic area. Scott had run off to find Ms. Myers over by the wigwams. Team Shawnee had followed Blacksmith Todd to the stables to see how horses got shod. Team Illini had disappeared inside the bake house.

It was just me and Mrs. Hunter and Mary Kay.

I guess Mary Kay's great friends at Walnut Knolls, the ones she'd chosen instead of me when she'd decided she didn't want to be my friend anymore because I was so "immature" for keeping a book of rules, weren't so great after all.

They had run off and deserted her just because there was a (remote) chance they might get stung by a bee if they stuck around!

"It's all right, Mary Kay," I said, reaching out to take her hand. "I'll go with you."

"No," Mary Kay said. She wouldn't budge. She just kept crying. "Not *you*."

This wasn't exactly a surprise. Even if it did hurt my feelings a little. I mean, I had never been anything but nice to Mary Kay. In my opinion, anyway.

I reminded myself that she'd just been stung by a bee — in the face — and probably wasn't thinking rationally.

"But I'm your buddy for the day," I reminded her. "Remember? So I *have* to come with you. Besides, it'll be fun. An adventure, just like everything else we've done today. We'll get to see what the inside of an office at a living history museum looks like!"

Even though her chin must have hurt a lot from being stung by a bee, and she was crying and mad at all her friends for ditching her, Mary Kay couldn't help cracking a little smile at that.

"You're such a d-dork sometimes, Allie," she said through her tears.

"Yeah," I said, tugging on her hand. "I know. I like dorky stuff. Like rules. But you like dorky stuff, too, Mary Kay. Or at least you used to. Like Barbie."

"Do you like Barbie, Mary Kay?" Mrs. Hunter asked lightly.

To my relief, Mary Kay finally started to move. I guess she realized she didn't have much of a choice. Mrs. Hunter led us toward where Master Baker Sean had pointed, a white building over by where the school bus was parked.

"I used to," Mary Kay said. She wasn't crying quite so hard now. "A long time ago. Like in the third grade." She shot me an annoyed look. "You're not *still* going on about that, are you, Allie? That's so immature."

Mary Kay sounded exactly like a mini Brittany.

You would have thought some of Brittany's glamour might have worn off since she'd ditched Mary Kay in her hour of need.

Oh, and started a war between our two schools.

But I guess not.

Mrs. Hunter opened the door to the Honeypot Prairie administrative office for us, and a rush of cool air-conditioning met us, along with a lady who wasn't dressed in old-timey clothes. "Oh, hello," she said with a smile. "Can I help you?"

Mrs. Hunter explained why we were there, and the lady, whose name was Miss Brown, led Mary Kay to a back room where she could lie down with a cool cloth over her face. Miss Brown gave her some ice to press to her chin, and got out the first aid kit with the EpiPens, just in case.

Then, while Mrs. Hunter called Mary Kay's mom — who asked to speak to Mary Kay, of course — I sat down and tried not to eavesdrop (because eavesdropping is wrong) on Mary Kay and her mom's conversation.

"But *why* won't you come pick me up?" I could hear Mary Kay asking her mom from the back room. "No, the bee sting's not that bad. I just want to come home. You don't understand. Brittany and those guys are being really *mean* again. . . ."

Again? So Brittany and Lauren and Paige had been mean to Mary Kay *before?* I wasn't the *only* one they were mean to? This was very interesting to know.

"Thank you, Allie," Mrs. Hunter said to me, coming to sit in the chair beside mine. I acted like I hadn't been eavesdropping (even though of course I had been), sitting up straight in my chair. "For being so kind to Mary Kay. I didn't know when I assigned you to be buddies for the day that the two of you had a . . . past. I'm sorry if that caused you any sort of discomfort."

"Oh," I said. I could feel myself blushing. Mary Kay and I had a past, all right.

A pretty bad one.

Especially when it came to field trips.

"That's okay," I said.

The funny thing was, I wasn't lying *or* acting when I said that. I really meant it. It *was* okay. Coming on this field trip to Honeypot Prairie — even as weird and sort of not fun as it had been — had finally made me feel like I was ready to move on from my past . . . not just my bad luck with field trips, but my past with Mary Kay and Brittany, too.

As I thought about this, I tried not to notice the way Mrs. Hunter's new engagement ring was catching the afternoon sunlight that was pouring through the office's plate-glass windows.

"What you did for her was very brave," Mrs. Hunter went on. "She's lucky to have you as a friend."

Ha! I was pretty sure Mary Kay wouldn't agree with that.

"And thank you, too," Mrs. Hunter said, "for what you did for Joey. I noticed how kind you were to him today . . ."

This made me blush even harder. I hoped Mrs. Hunter knew I had only helped Joey because it was my job as a positive influence, *not* because I liked him!

". . . though sometimes I worry Joey's never going to learn to stand up for himself if we don't let him fight his own battles from time to time," she went on.

This came as a surprise. I couldn't believe Mrs. Hunter, who'd assigned me to the back row of Room 209 to be a positive influence, was basically telling me I should have gone on a walkabout on Joey. . . .

So was I supposed to have just *let* people kick dirt on him and call him Upchuck?

Was Cheyenne just supposed to have *let* Brittany say those mean things about Pine Heights?

Oh, why did everything have to be so complicated?

Even though I felt more confused than ever, I did have to admit it felt very grown-up to be having this discussion with Mrs. Hunter in this office-y place, sitting in these grown-up chairs with Miss Brown typing away on her computer keyboard in the background, and Mrs. Hunter's engagement ring winking in the sunlight, and Mary Kay talking on Mrs. Hunter's cell phone, saying things like, "But, Mom, I don't *want* to," and "Mom. You don't *understand*."

It felt so grown-up, I felt like it would be okay if I asked a grown-up question.

"Mrs. Hunter," I said shyly. "Is that an engagement ring?"

I pointed at the ring on the third finger of her left hand, the one that was winking in the sunlight.

I was pretty sure I knew the answer already.

But I just wanted to know for sure.

Mrs. Hunter looked surprised. Then she smiled and touched her ring and said, "Why, yes, Allie. Yes, it is."

I looked down at my feet. I didn't really want to ask what I did next, because I was afraid of what the answer was going to be.

But I felt like I sort of had to. Because the dread of not knowing for sure was kind of worse than what her answer could be.

"So," I said, "does that mean you're going to be moving away?"

Mrs. Hunter sounded even more surprised.

"No," she said. "Of course not. Whatever gave you the idea that I was going to be moving?"

"Well," I said. "Because that man who threw the rocks at our windows had a suitcase. And if he was the old friend who sent you flowers —"

"Oh," Mrs. Hunter said with a laugh. "My goodness. Yes, that was David. He does live out of town, but he just got a job here for the city planning commission. So I'm not going anywhere."

I felt as if a giant weight had been lifted off my shoulders. Really.

It was almost like I'd gotten my own cell phone and Mewsie back, all in one.

Except not, of course. All that would have been way too good to be true.

"Well," I said, super relieved. "That's good."

Then the door to the office opened and Ms. Myers came in.

"I'm so sorry," Ms. Myers said. She was out of breath. "I was all the way out by the wigwams. Is she all right?"

"She's fine," Mrs. Hunter said with a smile, standing up. "She's talking to her mother right now. I'm afraid she wants to go home."

"Of course she does," Ms. Myers said, rolling her eyes. Then she noticed me and smiled and said, "Oh, Allie. Hello. I didn't see you sitting there."

"Hi, Ms. Myers," I said. I wasn't sure what to do exactly.

But I felt like I should do *something* to try to help the situation. I was so happy that Mrs. Hunter wasn't moving —

and thought I was brave, and had thanked me for being so kind . . . even if she thought I should let Joey fight his own battles from time to time — I'd have been willing to do *anything*. . . .

Even something I really didn't want to do.

"Do you want me to go talk to Mary Kay?" I volunteered. "Maybe I can convince her to stay."

Ms. Myers's face brightened. "Would you mind trying, Allie? That would be great. You two were always such good friends, and you've always been such a good influence on others. . . ."

"Thanks," I said. I was blushing again, but this time it was with pleasure. My mom may not have thought I was responsible enough to own a cell phone, but not just one but *two* of my teachers thought I was a good influence!

That had to count for something.

Mary Kay put Mrs. Hunter's phone down when she saw me in the doorway. "Yes?" she asked in a snotty way.

The red bump on her chin was enormous. Really.

"Hey," I said brightly. "Sorry to interrupt. But are you

ready to go back now? Because I figured you've had a long enough rest, and we're missing all the best stuff. The horse shoeing and the wigwam building, or whatever."

"I can't go back," Mary Kay said, her eyes filling with tears again. "*Look* at me."

"You look great," I lied. Because *You should always lie and tell someone they look great when they've just been stung in the face by a bee.* Total rule.

"Really?" Mary Kay sounded skeptical.

Lucky for me there were no mirrors in the back room, so she couldn't see herself.

"Oh, yeah," I said. "You can hardly notice it at all."

Mrs. Shiner said something on the phone. Mary Kay held it up to her ear and said, "*Okay,* Mom! Fine!"

Then she hung up.

"My mom has an important deposition," Mary Kay said, sitting up. "She says the bus is going to be leaving soon, so it's stupid for her to drive all the way out here to pick me up when I'm just going to be coming home in an hour or two, anyway."

"Well," I said. "It *is* kind of stupid. I mean, it's just a bee sting. Think what the early settlers went through in the eighteen fifties with all those wild boars and stuff. Way, way worse."

"But this isn't *really* the eighteen fifties," Mary Kay said, giving me a very sarcastic look. "I could be home, watching *Hannah Montana*."

"Yeah," I said. "But then you'd miss out on all the Team Shawnee fun."

"Right," Mary Kay said with a snort.

We looked at each other for a minute.

"I'm sorry," Mary Kay said finally.

Those were the last two words I ever expected to hear out of her mouth.

"Well," I said. "I'm sorry, too."

I didn't know what I was apologizing for, exactly.

But *When you've been fighting with a friend for so long you can barely remember why anymore, and she suddenly says she's sorry, you should say you're sorry, too.* That's another rule.

Mary Kay must have thought something along these

lines, since she looked at me with her eyes all narrowed and suspicious.

"Was the reason you stayed with me after I got stung," Mary Kay asked, "just because you had to, because you got assigned to be my buddy?"

"Well," I said. Why *had* I stayed with Mary Kay after she'd been stung? It wasn't like she'd been very nice to me today, or any other day. Actually, she'd been pretty mean to me every day I'd ever known her.

But that didn't matter. Wouldn't I have stayed with anybody, under the same circumstances? Because that's the rule? *Don't go on a walkabout on people who are in distress?*

Only I couldn't tell Mary Kay that, because that would have just hurt her feelings.

And she'd been hurt enough for one day.

And it's okay to lie if it means someone's feelings won't get hurt.

"No," I answered finally. "It's because I'm your friend."

Mary Kay looked really happy to hear this. Even though she'd never been too thrilled to be my friend before now.

Then she said, "Well. Let's go, then. Like you said, we don't want to miss out on the best stuff."

I smiled.

And we went to go find the rest of Team Shawnee.

RULE #19

If You Don't Work Together, You'll Never Finish Your Wigwam

It took so long to get to the stables from the administrative offices that Mary Kay and I missed Blacksmith Todd's forge demonstration, where he stuck pieces of metal into a very hot furnace and melted it (apparently, this was quite a popular demonstration, especially with the boys).

But we got there in time to see him put the shoe he'd made from the molten metal onto the horse.

It's hard to believe the nails going in doesn't hurt the horse. But it doesn't, Blacksmith Todd assured us. It's no different than getting your toenails cut. In fact, horses need to wear shoes to protect their feet just like we do.

Blacksmiths, we learned, were very important in the 1800s, like car mechanics are today, not only because they shod all the horses — which was the main way people got around in olden times — but because they made practically everything else back then, too, like frying pans and even guns (Patrick found this part particularly interesting). You couldn't just go to Target or Walmart and buy one, because there were no stores like those in olden times. You had to go to a blacksmith and have whatever you wanted made.

Blacksmith Todd did his best to bring Team Shawnee together with his talk about the importance of men who had his job in olden times.

But it was clear from the moment Mary Kay and I showed up that things on our team had been severed beyond repair.

All the Pine Heights kids were standing on one side of the stable, and all the Walnut Knolls kids were standing on the other. Even the size of Mary Kay's swollen chin — which was amazing — wasn't enough to unite them.

It took a visit to Mistress Carol and the authentic replica of a Native American wigwam she was in charge of making us build to do that.

Because by that time everyone was so mad at one another, a total fight broke out.

"You're not doing it right!" Lenny Hsu was yelling. "Hold them straight!"

"We *are* holding them straight," Paige said, referring to the sapling branches we were holding and that we were supposed to form into a structure that would eventually house all of us (once we covered the sapling branches with mats, which would keep out the rain we were supposed to pretend was coming).

"This is going to take *forever*," Cheyenne said, holding her sapling branch in place while Lenny and Scott scrambled around inside the wigwam, binding them together with string.

Cheyenne was right. Also, it was totally hot out. And there were more bees.

"You're doing so well," Mistress Carol assured us. Mistress Carol had been the lady I'd seen in the parking lot who'd been dressed the strangest out of all the prairie people. She had on a long skirt and a corset thingie on the outside, and all her waist-length hair was flowing free. She was also wearing a ton of necklaces. "I can *feel the positive energy* coming from you, children! You'll have this wigwam built in no time!"

"No, we won't," Cheyenne said, giving Mistress Carol a sour look. "Because we're going to have to leave to catch our bus in half an hour. And there's no way it's going to be finished by then."

"Ow," Lauren shrieked at Joey, letting go of her branch. "You stepped on my finger!"

And that's when the fighting started for real.

"*He* did it!" Brittany yelled, pointing at Joey. "Chuck did! It's all his fault!"

"Stop calling him Chuck," I yelled. "It's not his name!"

"I didn't mean to," Joey said to Lauren. "I'm sorry about your finger."

"Come on now," Mistress Carol said. "If you don't work together, you'll never finish your wigwam."

"None of this would be happening," Cheyenne shouted at Brittany, "if you all weren't such stuck-up snobs!"

"Stop," Mistress Carol said, grabbing Brittany's wrist, then Cheyenne's, and holding on to them. "All of you, stop. Just stop a moment, and stand still. Take a breath. Breathe. In. Out. In. Out."

We all stood where we were in the skeleton of our team's wigwam and did what Mistress Carol said. We breathed. In and out. In the distance, I could hear birds chirping in the treetops. And the far-off drone of more bees.

"Now," Mistress Carol said. "Sit. Wherever you are. Just sit."

Cheyenne looked down at the ground. "But my mother rented this period costume from New York and if I get it wrinkled it will cost thirty dollars to hand-press each individual —"

"Just sit," Mistress Carol said, and she yanked Cheyenne to the ground with her.

We all sat. Including Cheyenne. Even though she didn't look too happy about it.

"In the days when the Shawnee and the Pawnee and the Illini and the Miami Indians actually lived in this area," Mistress Carol said, sitting cross-legged with her eyes

closed, "they had a practice from which I believe you children could learn a thing or two. It was when some of the
members of the tribe — often around your age — would
come together for a sort of spiritual quest. . . ."

"You mean like a walkabout?" I asked in surprise.

Mistress Carol opened one of her eyes and looked at me.
"No," she said. "That's Australian."

"Oh," I said, disappointed.

"I'm talking about building a wigwam," Mistress Carol
said, closing her eyes again. "Just like those children from
ancient times, each one of you has weaknesses and strengths.
None of you is perfect. And just like those children from
ancient times, each one of you has to learn to work with
one another in order to help overcome your own weaknesses and make the most of your strengths, until you've
all achieved your goal. Of course, you could let petty bickering and closed mindedness stand in your way, so your
wigwam will never get built. Or you could open your heart
and mind and just accept one another's differences and
build the most amazing wigwam you can in the limited
time we have left. Which is it going to be?"

Open my heart and mind, I thought.

"I can't hear you," Mistress Carol said.

"Open our hearts and minds," a few of us murmured.

"It's funny," Mistress Carol said. "I still can't hear you."

"OPEN OUR HEARTS AND MINDS," we all said.

"Well, there," Mistress Carol said, opening her eyes and getting up. "Wasn't that simple? And now I want you to stand up and work *together* to finish your wigwam, keeping your hearts and minds open to each of your unique differences, which are what make you such amazing individuals. Because if you can do that, Team Shawnee, you can do *anything.*"

I didn't think it was going to work.

All Mistress Carol had done, after all, was make us sit on the ground while she gave a speech about keeping our hearts and minds open. She hadn't even had us walk through a thirteen-foot-tall working *model* of a heart, so we could see the way the ventricles and arteries worked, or anything like that. If you really want to open your heart, that would be the way to go about it, if you ask me.

But for some reason, we finished that wigwam, anyway. Lauren didn't argue any more with Joey about stepping on her finger. Lenny didn't yell at us for not keeping the branches straight. Cheyenne didn't even complain about how the whole thing was taking forever.

Of course, our wigwam didn't look very good. It looked awful, in fact. If it rained, no way would we have stayed dry. Our wigwam would have melted away.

But when it was done, we could all fit inside it. It was kind of cool, crouching inside our wigwam, shoulder to shoulder, looking out at Honeypot Prairie through the branches we'd twisted together ourselves.

It was kind of like being inside the SpaceQuest planetarium. Except it wasn't a planetarium. And it didn't have a Dinosphere.

But we'd made it ourselves. Without killing one another. While keeping our hearts and minds open to each of our unique differences, which were what made us such amazing individuals.

It was funny, but I doubted we could have learned *that* in a planetarium.

When Team Shawnee got on the bus, we were all feeling like one big, happy family.

"Give me your cell number," Dominique was saying to Lauren.

"Ooooh, give me yours," Lauren was saying.

"I'm going to have a sleepover," Brittany was saying. "And you're all invited."

"I can't wait," Cheyenne squealed.

"Wait," Scott was saying to Joey. "I thought you said it was faux fur."

"No," Joey said. "I just said that so the girls wouldn't get upset. It's real fur. My uncle shot and skinned it when he was a kid."

"Sweet," Paul Schmitt said. "Can I touch it?"

"No," Joey said. "Hands off the hat."

"Oh, no!" Mary Kay caught a glimpse of her reflection in the rearview mirror of the bus. "That's how I look? I look *awful*! Allie, why didn't you tell me?"

She burst into tears and wouldn't speak to me anymore.

I guess no matter how much you open your mind to one

another's unique differences, some things will never really change.

"Allie, Allie," Sophie cried, pulling me down next to her as I was going down the bus aisle. I'd been heading back toward the same seat I'd shared with Rosemary on the way to Honeypot Prairie.

But Sophie had other ideas for me.

"Will you talk to Erica, please?" she begged.

"Why?" I asked. "What's wrong with Erica?"

Erica was sitting next to the window, crying uncontrollably.

"It was j-just," she sobbed, "so w-wonderful!"

"What was?" I asked her bewilderedly.

"The whole thing," Erica said. "The field trip! Mrs. Higginbottom. Master Baker Sean. Mistress Carol. The horses. Didn't you love it? I don't want it to end, ever! I wish I could go back in time and live in the eighteen fifties!"

I guess I could understand why Erica had such a good time. I mean, she hadn't had Brittany, Cheyenne, Patrick, and Stuart on her team. Not to mention Mary Kay.

I wondered what Honeypot Prairie must have been like

from Erica's point of view. Obviously, totally magical —
like Narnia — if she was crying *that* hard because she didn't
want to go home.

"See?" Sophie whispered to me, shaking her head. "I told
you. You have to talk to her. She's nuts. I mean, it was fun,
but not *that* fun."

I was relieved someone else had some perspective on the
whole thing.

"Oh, my gosh, you guys," Caroline said, her head and
shoulders popping over the seat back in front of ours.
Elizabeth Pukowski joined her. "Was that amazing
or what?"

"It was certainly . . . interesting," I said.

"Interesting?" Caroline echoed. "It was fantastic! Wasn't
that the best bread you ever had? I'm going to get a cook-
book so I can learn how to make bread like Master
Baker Sean."

"Well," Sophie said. "I'm totally taking a first aid course
in case anyone is ever stung by a bee like that again and
needs medical aid. That way I'll be ready. Like Mrs.
Hunter was."

Caroline looked at her funny. "What are you talking about?"

"Oh, right!" Sophie cried. "You weren't there! Well, that friend of Allie's, Mary Kay —"

And she started telling Caroline and Elizabeth all about Mary Kay's bee sting.

I was sitting there kind of zoning out, thinking about all the strange things that had happened during the day, and how different they must have seemed from other people's perspectives, when all of a sudden someone said my name, and I looked up, and it was Mrs. Hunter.

"Here," she said with a smile. "You forgot this."

And she handed me my backpack.

"Oh," I said. "Thanks so much!"

I couldn't believe I'd been so irresponsible as to forget it.

"I think you'll find there's a surprise inside the front pocket," she said with a wink, before going to take her seat. "For being such a help today."

Not knowing what she could be talking about, I felt inside the front pocket . . .

. . . and pulled out a couple of folded sheets of paper. When I opened them, I saw that they were photocopies of George Washington's *Rules of Civility & Decent Behavior in Company and Conversation.*

I felt an electric jolt of excitement go through me.

"Oh, wow!" I cried, looking around for someone to show. But everyone was busy talking — or crying.

No one, I realized, would care as much as me.

Except for Mrs. Hunter. It was *just like her* to know that I would care . . . and to remember!

I folded the rules up and put them back in my backpack pocket.

Not because I didn't want to read them all right away . . .

. . . but because the bus had started, and reading while the car is going always makes me feel sick.

And you never want to be the person to throw up on the bus.

RULE #20

Don't Start What You Can't Finish

The bus ride from Honeypot Prairie wasn't anything like the bus *to* Honeypot Prairie. No one threw up.

No one was mean or sang songs about other people.

No one talked at all, hardly.

People seemed to be really worn out. A few people, like Mary Kay and Erica, cried. Lots of people, like Rosemary and Joey, slept.

When we got to Walnut Knolls Elementary and the kids from there started getting off the bus, some people (okay, Cheyenne) acted as if their hearts were breaking, and they were never going to recover.

"Text me!" Cheyenne screamed out the window at Brittany and Lauren and Paige.

"We will!" they all screamed back.

"They were just so *nice*," Cheyenne said to M and D, who agreed.

It is amazing how short some people's memories are.

And how long other people's are.

Mary Kay wasn't speaking to me again, because I hadn't told her how big the bee sting on her chin really was.

But that was okay. I'm pretty used to Mary Kay not speaking to me by now.

I knew she'd get over being mad. Someday.

"Keep it real," Scott Stamphley told Joey Fields, who barked sleepily at him.

Scott didn't say anything to Cheyenne as he walked off the bus, even though she said, *"Bye, Scott,"* in a very drippy manner that made me want to gag.

But he said, "Smell ya later, Stinkle," to me, and tugged *very* hard on one of my braids as he went by, then winked.

Sophie told me this was an unequivocal sign that he liked me.

"I don't think so," I said, rubbing my head.

"Oh, no," Sophie said. "I can guarantee it."

But pulling a girl's hair is not the same as throwing rocks at her classroom window and then sending her roses and giving her a diamond engagement ring.

So if Scott likes me he has a lot to learn.

As we all walked home from school after the bus let us off, I told Sophie, Erica, and Caroline what I'd learned about Mrs. Hunter and her fiancé. They were completely in awe of me, not to mention my superior detective skills.

"He's going to work for the city planning commission?" Sophie asked, wrinkling her nose. "That's so boring!"

"No, it's not," Caroline said. "That's a very important place to work. Those people . . . plan things. For the city."

"It would be more romantic if he was a doctor," Sophie said. "For sick children in a country where they don't have running water —"

"But he's not," Caroline said. "He works for the city planning commission. That's a good job, too. Not every job has to be romantic. Maybe he has other qualities. We know he's funny. Maybe he bakes bread. Did she say he bakes bread?"

"No," I said. "But he's probably smart, if he works for the city planning commission. I bet he can learn how, if Master Baker Sean learned how."

We'd reached the stop sign where we always separate to go to our different streets . . . Caroline and Sophie to theirs, and me and Erica to ours.

"Oh, my gosh," Sophie said. "I just remembered, Allie. I hope Mewsie is all right."

I felt a twist of nervousness in my stomach. I couldn't believe, in all the excitement about the field trip, I'd sort of forgotten about Mewsie.

"I hope so, too," I said, not really holding out much hope.

"He will be," Caroline said, handing me the nightgown I'd loaned her. "He's a good cat."

But being a good cat doesn't have anything to do with not being walled alive in someone's house.

I knew she was just trying to make me feel better. That's what friends do for one another.

"Thanks," I said, and gave her, then Sophie, hugs good-bye.

When Erica and I got closer to my house, I could see the A+ Roofing van in the driveway and the men on top of the roof.

"Well," Erica said, "that's a good sign."

"Why?" I asked.

"Well, if there were something wrong with Mewsie, your mom and dad probably would have sent A-Plus Roofing home."

I didn't think Erica knew my mom and dad very well. But I said, "You're probably right."

"Today was such a good day," Erica said with a happy sigh, "there's no way anything bad could have happened to Mewsie to ruin it."

I thought Erica was maybe suffering from field trip overload. But I hugged her good-bye in my front yard, anyway, gave her her mom's apron back, and said, "I'm sure you're right!" and tried to believe that she was right all the way up the stairs to the front porch and through my front door, ignoring the fact that we're supposed to use the side door through the mudroom . . .

. . . because you can get upstairs much faster if you go through the front door of my house.

"HiI'mhome," I yelled very fast, throwing my backpack down at the bottom of the stairs, then taking the steps two at a time to the second floor.

"Hi, honey," I heard Mom calling from somewhere in the house. "How was your field trip? Did you have a nice time? Oh, Allie, don't leave your things spilled all over the bottom of the stairs. I built you kids those nice cubbies in the mudroom for you to put your things in, why won't you ever . . ."

But I had already burst into Mark's room and flung myself onto the floor of his closet, my face smushed in front of the hole in the wall.

"Mewsie!" I called. "Oh, Mewsie! Here, kitty, kitty, kitty!"

He *had* to come out, I told myself. He just *had* to. Everything else had worked out . . . Joey. Mrs. Hunter. Mary Kay (well, sort of).

Even Brittany and Cheyenne had worked out their

differences. And during that wigwam thing with Mistress Carol, I'd felt like . . . well, I'd sort of felt like *neither* of them were all that bad at heart, once you got to know them, and they stopped playing their stupid games and started acting normal, for a change.

So why couldn't this *one thing* work out, too?

"Allie," Mom said from the doorway. She didn't look too happy.

"Mom," I said. There were tears in my eyes. I had held them in all day, and not cried once — well, except when Scott had yanked on my braid so hard — even though I'd really *wanted* to cry a couple of times.

But now I just couldn't hold my tears in any longer.

"I *can't* go put my backpack away right now," I said. "I have to get Mewsie out of the wall. I know you're very disappointed in me because I've been so irresponsible. But I was actually *very* responsible today on the field trip. You can ask Mrs. Hunter if you don't believe me. Mary Kay got stung by a bee, and I'm the *only one* who stuck by her, even though everyone else ran away because they were afraid they might get stung. I walked her to the office and sat with her and everything. And you know I can't stand Mary Kay. And I didn't trade to get off the team I got assigned because I didn't want to leave Joey Fields alone when everyone was picking on him, even though I don't even like Joey Fields." I was crying when I said all this. "And it's okay, because I don't even want a cell phone anymore. All I want is for Mewsie to be out of the wall. Okay? That's *all I want.*"

"Well," Mom said. "In that case, you might want to go see what's sitting on your bed."

I just stared up at her through my tears.

"What?" I asked. "Why?"

"Go look," Mom said, and held Mark's bedroom door open for me.

Not sure what to expect, I got up off the floor and walked past Mom, out of Mark's bedroom, and across the hall to mine.

There, sitting on my bed, licking himself, sat Mewsie.

I screamed with happiness and ran to pick him up. I kissed him all over . . . even though he was covered in chips of wood and tiny snail shells and pieces of something I'm pretty sure were the same mushrooms that had been all over Kevin when he'd crawled out of the hole.

And truthfully, Mewsie didn't seem that glad to see me. He kept making grunting noises and even growling a little because I was squeezing him so tightly.

I didn't care.

I was just so happy to have him back from his walkabout!

"When did he come out?" I asked Mom tearfully. Only now they were tears of happiness.

"A little while ago," she said. "I think he knew it was time for you to come home from school, so he came out to wait for you."

When she said this, I had to give Mewsie more kisses. He was the best cat ever!

Even if he'd been very, very naughty.

"I told Mark to keep his door shut from now on," she said, "to keep Mewsie out until we can get the wall repaired."

"Thanks, Mom," I said, putting Mewsie down. Because

even though I wanted to go on squeezing him, he was growling pretty unhappily.

Plus, he really was very dirty from being inside the hole.

"So," Mom said. "I guess after all that I don't even have to ask how Honeypot Prairie was. That bad, huh?"

I thought about it.

"It wasn't as fun as the Children's Museum would have been," I said finally. "But I think I learned a lot of new stuff. Like, did you know that President Washington kept a book of rules when he was a kid? Mrs. Hunter made a copy of them and gave it to me as a reward for sitting with Mary Kay after she got stung by the bee."

Mom smiled.

"Well," she said, "that was nice of her. But learning new stuff is actually the point of field trips, Allie."

I had never thought about it this way before. I had sort of always thought of field trips as just being about having fun.

"Yeah," I said. "I guess it sort of is."

Mom reached out and hugged me.

"Listen," she said. "It sounds like you took on a lot of responsibility during this field trip."

"Yeah," I said. "I really did."

I felt a glimmer of hope. Was she going to —

"I still don't think you're quite old enough to handle a cell phone right now," she said.

"Aw, *Mom*," I said, my hopes crushed.

"But sixth grade is an awfully long way away," Mom said. "What do you think about fifth grade?"

Fifth grade? Fifth grade was next year! Not even a year. Just one summer vacation away!

"Really?" I asked, brightening. "I can spend my money on a cell phone?"

"Save your money," Mom said with a laugh. "Dad and I will foot the bill. Now go put your backpack away in your cubby in the mudroom."

My heart filled with happiness, I ran to go do what she'd asked. I couldn't believe my good fortune.

But later, as I was pinning President Washington's rules to my bulletin board — where I'd be sure to see them first thing every morning and last thing every night — I realized I shouldn't have been so surprised by how well everything had turned out.

Especially when I noticed Rule the Eighty-second: *Undertake not what you cannot Perform, but be Careful to keep your Promise.*

Because this was exactly what I'd done: I'd made a promise — to myself — the night before that if Mewsie turned out to be okay, I wouldn't complain anymore (or at least, not as much). I'd also promised not to be irresponsible.

And today during the field trip, I'd been *super* responsible.

And look what had happened!

Don't start what you can't finish. Always keep your promises.

And okay, true, I still might complain sometimes. And I might even still be irresponsible.

But that's why I had the rules: to remind me when I messed up!

Maybe, I thought to myself, old things — like wigwams, one-room schoolhouses, interactive history museums, and

President Washington's rules — weren't so bad after all. Without them, we wouldn't know how good we have it in the present.

Like, if I wasn't friends with Mary Kay, I wouldn't appreciate what great friends I have in Erica, Caroline, and Sophie.

And if I didn't have the Allie of the past to compare myself to, I wouldn't know how great the new and improved Allie is!

The truth was, I'd decided that I liked her already.

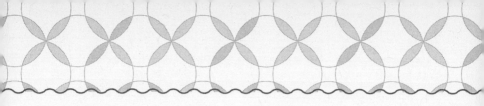

- No cell phones until you're in the sixth grade.
- It's important to be nice to your neighbors.
- Losing electronic devices is irresponsible.
- Ignorance of the law is no excuse.
- No one goes in the wall.
- Moms don't snap too often. But when they do, you had better stop whatever you were doing wrong, if you know what's good for you.
- If you've earned the money, you should be able to spend it on whatever you want.
- If you have to walk your little brother to and from kindergarten every day, you should be considered responsible enough to have a cell phone.
- Cheyenne O'Malley is the most popular girl in Room 209, and probably in the whole world . . . at least in her own mind.
- When a teacher like Mrs. Hunter says she has an announcement, you know it's going to be something exciting.
- Asking teachers about their boyfriends is against the rules.

- Don't trust something important (such as handing in a permission slip) to somebody flaky (and mean).
- If there's going to be a field trip and Allie Finkle is scheduled to go on it, you can just count her out.
- Boys do weird things to show girls that they like them, such as try to wipe boogers on them.
- Living history museums are just awful.
- Extra credit is always nice to have, just in case.
- When you're feeling bad, the worst thing you can do is inflict your bad mood on others.
- Never go to a birthday party given by the most popular girl in your old school just because her mother has rented a limo to take you there. It will NOT turn out well.
- If you don't keep wounds clean, they could become infected, and then might become gangrenous and you could die.
- If you want to fix the leaks and kill the dry rot going on inside your walls, you're going to have to replace a lot of shingles.
- No slamming doors.

- You should never read other people's private correspondence.
- It's all good practice for when you're famous.
- It's always better to lie if that lie makes someone feel better.
- If you went somewhere and had a terrible time, maybe tone it down a little when you're describing it to people later, or they might blow it out of proportion, and then it could come back to haunt you.
- It's very rude to call someone a troglodyte.
- You can't wear a nightgown to school.
- No Finkle kid can go on the roof.
- Nothing else matters when you've lost the one thing you care about more than anything else in the whole world.
- None of us has any idea how truly awful things can get.
- Anyone who would fall for Kevin's cute face is not to be trusted.
- All that matters are the people — and pets — you love.
- Make sure your little brothers don't do stupid things.
- Never eat anything red.

- It's rude to tell someone they look like a French poodle. Unless they are, in fact, a French poodle.
- If you can't say something nice, just keep your mouth shut.
- The best way to keep people from talking about a certain subject is not to bring it up yourself.
- Old things bring nothing but trouble.
- Bullying is still wrong, even when it's being done to someone who is a bully herself.
- You can't have enough buddies.
- No getting up while the bus is in motion.
- No trading team assignments.
- If you're caught trading team assignments, the punishment will be severe.
- It's wrong to hate people.
- It's important to make a big entrance.
- Taking a walkabout when someone needs you is just about the most irresponsible thing you can do.
- Tattling on people is kind of mean. Unless it's for a good reason.

- Speak not injurious Words, neither in Jest nor Earnest.

- Every Action done in Company, ought to be with Some Sign of Respect, to those that are Present. (When you're in the company of others, you ought to be respectful and courteous of them.)

- When in Company, put not your Hands to any Part of the Body, not usually Discovered. (When you're with other people, do not stick your hands down your pants or your finger up your nose.)

- Show Nothing to your Friend that may affright him. (Don't scare your friends.)

- Use no Reproachful Language against any one, neither Curse nor Revile. (Don't be mean to people.)

- Appear calm in the face of a medical emergency.

- You should always lie and tell someone they look great when they've just been stung in the face by a bee.

- When you've been fighting with a friend for so long you can barely remember why anymore, and she suddenly says she's sorry, you should say you're sorry, too.

- Don't go on a walkabout on people who are in distress.

- It's okay to lie if it means someone's feelings won't get hurt.
- If you don't work together, you'll never finish your wigwam.
- You never want to be the person to throw up on the bus.
- Undertake not what you cannot Perform, but be Careful to keep your Promise. (Don't start what you can't finish. Always keep your promises.)